Liz

MW00620443

Remember Me

Hitter Squad Series
Novella

Please Enjoy!

Blue Saffire

*With Love,
Blue Saffire*

Perceptive Illusions Publishing, Inc.
Bay Shore, New York

Blue Saffire/Perceptive Illusions Publishing, Inc.
PO BOX 5253
Bay Shore, New York 11706
www.BlueSaffire.com

Publisher's Note: This is a work of fiction. Names, characters, places, and incidents are a product of the author's imagination. Locales and public names are sometimes used for atmospheric purposes. Any resemblance to actual people, living or dead, or to businesses, companies, events, institutions, or locales is completely coincidental.

Ordering Information:
Quantity sales. Special discounts are available on quantity purchases by corporations, associations, and others. For details, contact the "Special Sales Department" at the address above.

Remember Me: Hitter Squad Series Book 1/ Blue Saffire. -- 1st ed.
ISBN 978-1-941924-69-3

You define who you are, not their words.

—Blue Saffire

CHAPTER ONE

Hello

Dallas

I stumble out of the stall already piss drunk. It's been one of those nights. I never seek to find trouble but it has a way of always finding me. I'm used to it by now.

I'm sure my father is still cursing the day I was born. Well, fuck him and the day I was spit out of my mother's twat. They never gave a shit about me. That's why I am the way I am.

My life has been shit from day one. Who am I kidding? It's been bullshit from the womb. My mother never heeded a single warning label. Bitch smoked, drank, and God knows what else while pregnant with me. My father used to say the only reason I wasn't a crack baby was because I was too mean and ornery to be addicted to shit.

Mean.

That bastard had some nerve. I saw the sole of his boot to my head more times than I can count. It's a wonder I don't have brain damage.

They say, hurt people, hurt people. I believe that. I actually think it might be a law somewhere. I've had my fair share of hurt and it came from a whole lot of hurt people.

I've had one friend in my entire life. She was my neighbor's niece. We were so young I probably shouldn't even remember her. But I remember. I remember because she was the only one that was ever nice to me.

She never made me feel like I was dirty or stupid. Not like everyone else. I think I lost my last bit of humanity when I lost my one friend. To this day, I remember kicking and screaming trying to get to her as she was taken away.

She came and left every year, but I knew something was different this time. I'll never forgive my father for not letting me say goodbye. I'd bit his ass for holding me back in that trailer.

I watched through the dirty window as she drove away to who knows where. I guess she went back to whatever heaven she'd come from once a year. She didn't belong in the hell stained place I grew up in.

Those brown eyes have haunted me for years. I don't even know why I'm thinking of her now. I have bigger shit on my plate. Like where the fuck I'm going to get Skull his money from.

Only I would get myself into some shit like this. Hell, I shouldn't even be out here in the open drunk. There's a price on my head and it's going to get paid one way or another.

I just don't give a fuck anymore. Maybe I'm suicidal and that's why I haven't found a way out of this. It's the only logical explanation I can come up with.

Dallas Steel-Echoes, suicidal asshole. Has a ring to it. Also sounds about right. I can't get my shit together to save my life. Literally.

"Dallas, you got a call," Arty grunts across the bar as I stumble out of the bathroom.

My brows knit. Who the fuck would be calling me here? Shit, the trouble looking for me would just show up, not call. I pull my cell phone from my pocket. I don't have any missed calls.

My piece of shit old lady left my ass months ago. If that's that bitch calling, I have a bullet for her ass. All of this bullshit started because of her. Thieving ass bitch. I've been digging myself out of this hole since she made off, taking shit that wasn't mine to begin with.

I stagger to the bar to see who the fuck's on the phone. I signal for another beer but Arty rolls his fucking eyes at me and ignores me. Fuck him. I know my limit. I haven't reached it yet.

"Hello, who's this?" I grunt into the phone, surprising myself when I hear my words slur.

"Is this Dallas?"

I rock sideways as the sexiest voice I've ever heard pours through the line. I have to prop my hip against the stool beside me. Fuck the fact that some blonde is already sitting on it.

That voice. It's husky but soft. The type of shit that makes your dick hard. I bet the lips it's coming from are lush and nice to watch while sucking your cock.

"Yeah, this is Dallas. Who's this?"

"Anita," she says softly. "Do you remember me?"

My brows furrow. Only Anita I ever knew was the little girl that had once been my friend. I haven't seen or heard from her since I was ten.

I still remember her brown eyes, skin the color of dark honey, and dark hair that was always in all those plaits on her head. Her laughter has played in my head since I was a small boy. I never had anything to laugh about without her. Her musical chimes have been a background sound in my fucked up life to remind me what real joy is like. Or at least, what I believed it sounds like.

"Dallas? Are you there?" she asks when I don't reply.

"Yeah, I'm here," I nod as if she can see me.

"I need your help," she says with caution in her voice.

She should be cautious. Fucking with me only brings trouble. Anyone in their right mind would steer clear of me.

"I can't help my damn self. How am I supposed to help you?" I snarl into the phone.

"You have a problem. I can fix it. I help you, you help me," she says with more determination in her voice.

"Oh yeah? Well, how you plan to help me, sweetness? Honestly, my cock has been pretty dry. You plan on wetting it for me?" I chuckle into the phone.

Yup, told you I was an asshole. Besides, I don't know this woman. She can't help me do shit. If I'm going to die, I'm going to face that shit head on like a man. I'm not running to no pussy to save me.

"I can make that hundred thousand dollar price tag go away," she tosses out the hook that catches me right in the nose.

I'm listening. She has my full attention now. I even sober up just a bit.

"What do you know about that?" I hiss.

"I was contracted to collect the fee," she leaves the words hanging in the air.

Well shit, I'm not even worth a male assassin. What the hell? Did they plan on having her fuck me to death?

"What would you say if I told you I could make your problem go away and put another two million into your pocket?"

Her voice is absolutely becoming sweeter by the minute. If she keeps talking with all that sugar, I might be tempted to have a sip of the sweet tea she's selling. I'm so parched.

"Whatcha need to extend that hospitality, Darlin'?" I croon into the line.

"It's simple. Marry me."

I'm starting to feel like I'm being fucked with no lube. I swear all that innocence disappears as the words slip from her lips. This has to be a joke.

No one wanted me, let alone would be willing to pay to marry my ass. This chick has to be desperate or ugly as fuck. What kind of hitter was she anyway? Calling her mark to propose marriage.

"Think about it, Dallas. You have two days. Skull wants his money then. If you don't pay, then I come to town to pay you a visit. We both know you don't have what you owe.

"If you choose option A, I'll help make it all go away. And in the end, you'll have a nice nest egg to help you buy the biggest train set in the world," she purrs.

I stumble back almost falling on my ass. The real Anita is the only person in the world that knows I once said I wanted to be rich so I could buy the biggest train set ever made. This has to be her, but ain't shit adding up.

"How do I let you know if I want to take option A," I say, too stunned to process what the fuck is going on.

"Sober up. I'll find you," she says and ends the call.

I pull the receiver from my ear and stare down at it. *What the fuck?* I think I just walked into the twilight zone.

I toss the phone on the bar and turn to walk away. I'm moving away from the table my so-called buddies are surrounding. Anyone of them would slice my throat for the right price.

"Hey Dallas," I hear hollered behind me. "Where the hell you going?"

"To sober up," I holler back, not even bothering to turn around.

CHAPTER TWO

The Decision

Havana

My father thinks he's so slick. It's his damn fault I'm the way I am. I can't believe he would do this to me. If he weren't already dead, I'd put a fucking bullet in him.

My father always taught me, never trust an assassin. We're trained in the art of seduction, persuasion, and deception. Boy, did he deceive me.

Too bad I'll be the one getting the last laugh. I don't even know how he thought this would work. One year...I can do this for one year and then I'll be right back to doing what I was born and raised to do.

I'm a killer. I do what killers do. I put dirt bags to ground for a price. There hasn't been a man to date that didn't deserve the death I handed to them. I could smell their worthlessness from the time I received their names.

It was one of the reasons I took pause when the name Dallas Echoes was handed to me. The guy reeks of being a fuck up and an asshole, but not the kind of dirt bag that would warrant a visit from me. I do the worst of the worst, the scum of the earth. This guy isn't in my wheelhouse. I wouldn't even enjoy the hit.

After some digging, I found out my gut was right. Dallas, I remembered those eyes the minute I saw them, one hazel brown, one blue. As if God realized he had created perfection and decided to add a single flaw to be humorous. Humorous because even the one imperfection isn't enough to take away from the perfect specimen of a man.

I looked through every picture I could get my hands on of the mark I'm supposed to be after. Picture after picture revealed the fine ass man my little best friend had grown up to be. Rough around the edges? Yes. A bit dirty? Sure. But underneath all that dirt and grime is a sexy as sin man.

I remember Dallas's father. He was an asshole and a dirty bastard himself. It's no wonder Dallas grew up the way he did. I just never thought his name would find me. Hell, he's lucky it did.

He'd be dead in a week if it hadn't. I roll my eyes at the lame job. Once again my father's fault. He's killing me with this bullshit. I can't get a single decent hit.

I could once book double digit millions for a single job. Now, no one will answer my calls. I've been frozen out of the circle and this shit is going to get hot if I don't get some damn money soon.

I don't understand what my father was thinking. To leave me out here with nothing and no way to take care of myself. If I don't go through with this bullshit he's left in my lap there's bound to be a price on my head.

"Shit," I mutter, tossing a vase across the room.

My chest heaves, my eyes bounce around my home office. The mortgage is due. The two thousand dollar mortgage. I can't keep going like this. These cheap jobs are going to have me living in a box.

Literally, my finances are the least of my worries if I keep taking these jobs. It's frowned upon for a hitter of my stature to go on these rogue hits. They're the type of work that can expose too much.

Still, I have to do something. How am I supposed to pay the boys? My father fucked us all. They're going to start asking questions soon. I don't have work for them and I'm running out of money to cover up what my father has done.

It's been two months and I've tapped out all of my resources. My eyes burn with tears I'll never shed. I'm so frustrated. I've never had to rely on anyone. Now, I have placed my future in the hands of a certified fuck up.

If Dallas doesn't take the bait, I'll have no choice but to kill him and collect the weak ass ten grand. His ass owes more than that. *I* owe more than that.

For years, my father tried to get me to use my real estate license legitimately. That's only a front, but it looks like I may have to show up at the office for an honest day's work soon. We're all going to have to figure out how to settle in to our cover lives.

"Son of a bitch," I huff.

"Boss," I turn to see Aisha staring down at the broken glass on the floor.

Her brows pinch in concern. She's the only other person I've told about my father's betrayal and fuckery. When the boys start asking questions I need her to be on her toes. She's a shit liar, but with the right instructions she'll be able to help me hold them off a little longer.

"Yeah," I sigh, rubbing the tension out of my forehead.

"Mr. Echoes has been in his trailer for two days," she says after lifting her eyes and clearing her throat.

"You said he tossed all the alcohol the first night. Has he had a drink since?"

"No, ma'am, not from what I can see on the camera," she replies.

I shoot her a stern look. We're almost the same age and grew up like sisters. She shouldn't be calling me ma'am. I blow out a breath.

Good, he has made a decision.

"Tell the boys to pick him up. Under *no* circumstances are they to kill him," I say sharply.

"Is force allowed?" Aisha asks.

I roll my eyes. Telling the guys they can use force is like ordering a kill. Dallas is a big guy, but they'll beat him to within an inch of his life.

"No, I don't want a single hair harmed. They bring him in as clean as possible. Tell them exactly that. They'll understand."

I wave her away turning for the wall of windows in my office. Folding my arms across my chest, I inhale a deep breath. I love this house. I love my life. I'll do anything I have to, to keep it.

"Good luck," I mutter to myself. "Bastard has me by the balls. Dammit, Augustine, why'd you do this?"

Did you hate me after all?

~B~

Dallas

14

I've been sober for two days. Two days and nothing. I have one more day before all hell breaks loose. I feel like I've been played. Not a drop to drink and that bitch hasn't shown up.

"Let me get a bottle of Jack," I say to the store clerk, pointing to the fifth of whiskey.

If I'm going to die, I'm going out my way. My last attempt to get my hands on that money fell through this morning. I'm fucked. I might as well get lost in the bottom of a bottle.

I toss the last of my cash on the counter and snatch up the bottle. The clerk shoots me a disgusted look. He can kiss my filthy ass.

I wipe the back of my hand across my mouth. I haven't been this dry in months. I feel twitchy and it has nothing to do with the death dealer coming for me.

I step outside and screw the cap off the bottle as I head for my car. The squeal of tires pulls my attention just as I lift the bottle to my lips. I'm frozen with the bottle tilted toward my mouth.

A white van stops in front of me and the back door slides open. A big motherfucker jumps out, staring me down with his arms folded in front of him and a gun clinched in his right hand.

The bottle slips from my hand to the ground. I stiffen ready for a fight. He's going to have to earn the bullet hole he gets in me.

"Get in," he nods over his shoulder to the van.

"Fuck you," I hiss.

"Not my type. Get in the damn van," he grumbles.

I go to charge him, prepared to take a bullet as he lifts the gun. What I wasn't prepared for was the charge of electricity that runs through me. I convulse as I feel like I stuck a pair of scissors in a socket. This asshole is tasing me with a smile on his face.

I'm still convulsing when the driver gets out and the two of them toss my ass face down in the back of the van. Skull has always been an impatient asshole. I should've known he'd send someone early. What's a day or two to him? He knows I don't have his money.

"What does she want with his guy?" I hear one of the two goons say.

"Don't know. He's a filthy bastard though," the other answers.

"You don't think she's going to do anything stupid, do you?" the first one says.

"You really think she'd marry that stinking piece of shit? He smells like ass and corn chips," he replies.

"I don't know what she's thinking. Why hasn't she told us?"

"Pride, hurt, needing control," the second guys says.

"She could have come to one of us. Why not ask one of us?"

"We've all grown up together. The only thing that says we're not family is our blood. Do you really think she'd ask one of us to go through with this?"

"I have no idea what the old man was thinking."

"Tristan, I have no fucking clue. This could get us all killed," he sighs.

"Man, she can't be about to do what I think she is," Tristan huffs.

"His funky ass doesn't deserve her. Maybe she plans to use him then put a bullet in his head," the other guy mumbles.

"She'd have to throw his ass in bleach first," Tristan chuckles.

"Fuck you," I finally manage to push through my lips.

I hear a shuffle behind me, pulling my attention. A third guy, as big as the first two stares back at me with dark soulless eyes. They light up just before he smiles and punches the shit out of me. That manic smile is the last thing I see before it all goes dark.

CHAPTER THREE

Clean up

Havana

I roll my shoulders trying to release my anger. I tried to take Will's head off, after Tristan and Rich told me he was the one responsible for the bruise on Dallas's face. He's been knocked out since they arrived with him.

Why is it so hard for people to do as I ask?

"You're a big fella," I say under my breath as I walk over to the bathtub in my master bath.

I had Rich and Tristan begrudgingly strip Dallas and place him in a hot bath. He still hasn't regained consciousness, but he's breathing. He reeked. I couldn't wait for him to wake before we cleaned him up.

I squat beside the tub, placing my elbows on my knees, letting my arms dangle between my legs. My eyes are fixed on the giant in my tub with his head slumped to the side. Little Dallas is all grown up.

His dark hair is longish on the top. At the moment, it's greasy and spilling onto his forehead. The sides and back are tapered low.

None of the boy I knew remains in his face. His chiseled jaw line covered in scuff has erased all of that. Sitting before me is all man. My eyes travel down his body deeper into the tub. My brows shoot up.

"Well damn," I say appreciatively. "And that's at rest? Damn."

I force my eyes back up over his body, focusing on his face. For a drunk and a fuck up he's kept his body in good shape. He'll do well enough for what I need.

I reach for the sponge, dipping it into the water. Lifting it over his head I squeeze the warm liquid out. His eyes flash open and he begins to spatter.

A smile grows on my lips as those eyes lock on me. Simply gorgeous. Dallas Steel-Echoes is beauty personified.

~B~

Dallas

I think I've died and gone to heaven. The moment I look into those brown eyes I feel like I'm falling forward into their depths. It's when I look at that smile on her lips that I'm certain that I'm in the right place.

I didn't get into heaven. I went straight to hell and this is one of Satan's minions. Those lips promise nothing but sin. That smile is sinister with a hint of come-hither.

"Hello, Dallas," she purrs in that sexy ass voice from the phone.

I narrow my eyes at her. I'm not about to be fooled by that voice or her pretty face. I blink my wet lashes, trying to get the water out of my eyes. My head has a dull ache on the side.

"Where am I?" I grunt.

"My home," she shrugs.

She lifts a sponge, wiping the water out of my face. I watch her closely as she stands, shifting to sit on the edge of the tub. My cock twitches in the water. I've already mentally confirmed this is Anita.

A very grown up, sexy as fuck Anita. Everything about her is different, yet familiar. Her dark hair is now cut short like Halle Berry in Catwoman. All them curves are the curves of a woman you want to hold onto and get lost in. There's nothing skinny or rail thin about her. Not the type of woman I've had the pleasure of getting into.

That skin still looks like smooth dark honey. Her nose is still cute as a button. However, those lips—just as I thought while hearing her voice over the phone—I'd love to have them wrapped around me. Her eyes are the same, but not.

She's seen things since we were kids. The type of stuff that changes you to your core. The girl I knew was sweet and innocent. This woman before me is dangerous with secrets that are deadly. I don't doubt that for a second.

"Why am I here?" I grit through my teeth.

"You sobered up. I figured you were taking me up on my offer," she replies, tilting her head at me.

Something flashes in her eyes, something I just barely catch. Fear, concern, worry, it's one of the three if not a combination of them all. I zone in on her face, but it's impassive now. Just like that she's shutdown all emotion. It's an eerie trait on a woman. I'm not sure I like it or trust it.

I'm used to dealing with emotional women that wear their feelings in plain sight twenty four seven. I don't like not being able to read this woman sitting before me. Especially when sitting butt fucking naked in a tub, with my cock trying to think for me.

Her eyes lower to the water, obviously giving attention to the one calling for it. With that same blank expression, she reaches the hand holding the sponge into the water. My eyes drop to follow that hand.

It lifts from the water, moving to my head. Just as she reaches to place the sponge to my forehead my hands shoot up to grasp her wrist. It's once I have her locked in my hold that I realize my hands have been cuffed together.

Pissed off I tug her forward, but she uses her strength and her free hand to keep me from bringing her into the water with me. We lock eyes and a grin pushes up the corners of my lips. I've pulled a reaction from her.

Her ample chest heaves in my face, her nostrils flare, those lips purse and twist and her eyes flash with venom. I lick my lips. I like the fire I see rising up in her.

"You smell like shit," she hisses. "Release me so I can clean your funky ass up. If you don't, I'll break both of your hands and you'll be trying to wipe your ass with your elbows for months."

I flash her a smile, revealing all of my teeth. She rolls her eyes in disgust. I'm tempted to tug harder to get that body into this water with me but I know she's right. I reek.

I haven't showered in days. When you're trying to figure out where you're going to get a hundred grand to save your life, some things get forgotten or pushed to the side. Oh well.

Dead men don't need baths. I had no one to impress so it is what it is. I turn my head to sniff at my pit and frown.

"Damn," I mutter.

She snatches away from my hold. I turn back to watch her stand to her full height, glaring at me. Lifting my bound hands I push my hair back off my face.

"Still want to get married, Anita?" I chuckle.

"Havana," she snaps.

My brows draw. Her jaw works while I try to figure out what she's talking about. She draws in a breath seeming to calm herself. She rolls her neck, then her shoulders. Once again that lack of expression has been carefully put into place.

"My name is Havana," she says. "Never call me Anita. Anita doesn't exist anymore."

"Whatever you say, Anita," I taunt.

She gives me just the reaction I've been looking for. Her eyes flash with anger and her fists ball at her sides. I don't think she realizes she squeezing soapy water on the floor. Or maybe she just doesn't care.

"This may be a game to you, but let me make something clear. Your life is still in danger. Your debt is still owed, leaving that price on your head. This little show you're putting on. It'll get you a bullet right in the forehead. I don't have time to bullshit with you," she grinds out.

"Now, the way I see it. You need me just as much as I need you or else my dirty ass wouldn't be sitting in your nice white tub. So stop threatening me with bullets and shit," I growl back.

She tosses the sponge at my face, I duck out of the way letting it splash into the water. When my eyes lock on her, she has a pistol aimed at my head. My jaw ticks. With my hands bound in front of me, I know I won't be able to get up out of this tub as fast as I need to.

So I sit back and sink into the water as if she's not pointing a thing at me. I stare down the barrel of her gun, challenging her and death. At least if I die here, I can say I went out in luxury, something no one ever expected for me.

I piss her off more, when I lift my arms, placing my hands behind the back of my head. I let my eyes truly scan her body now that it's in my full view. Never dated a black woman before, but I'd give this one a go. She has to be five-five maybe five-six.

If I stood I'd tower over her by a good foot at least. My six-five would dwarf her. She's not wearing much of a top beneath her blazer, revealing a healthy amount of her salacious cleavage. My eyes take in her expensive suit and heels. It's clear that little Anita and I have grown up worlds apart.

I take the time to think this over. This bathroom screams money as much as the black pants suit draping that fit, thick body. Why would she need to marry me? With looks like hers she could have any man she wants. I'd fuck her in a heartbeat if I thought I was anywhere near worth her time.

Why go through all this trouble to make me her husband? She's not ugly as fuck, never has been. I only thought that might be the problem before I was certain this was my childhood friend. Now that I've confirmed this is Anita, she could have shaved her head bald, knocked out all her teeth, and tatted up every inch of that pretty brown skin and she'd still be the most beautiful woman I'd ever seen.

Something ain't right. Which leads me to my next conclusion. She's desperate. She's just as desperate as I am. For what, I don't know, but something has put this filly's back against the wall.

"For reasons I don't have time to explain to you, you're the option I've chosen. But don't think that makes you my only option," she says tightly.

"This shit ain't getting neither one of us nowhere. You said you can help me. So far, I've done what you asked only to be tased, knocked the fuck out, and cuffed naked as the day I was born, while turning into a prune in your bathtub. I'm not interested in dying, baby girl. So tell me…how do I help you so you can help me?"

I close my eyes and sigh. I'm bone tired. If she was going to pull that trigger she'd have done it already.

-B-

Havana

I drag my tongue over my teeth. I hate that this man has the ability to pull a reaction from me. Filthy, funky, and all, my pulse raced when he tugged me toward him.

He sees too much. Even as little kids he had a keen eye. People thought Dallas was stupid. He's not, never has been. It's one of the reasons I considered him for this.

I relax and tuck my gun back in the holster at the small of my back. It infuriates me that he's so relaxed. What gives him this type of confidence in my presence? I've brought fear to men ten times as powerful as he is.

I tamp down my raging thoughts. I need to secure this agreement before he pushes me to blow his head off. I unbutton my suit jacket, shrugging it off to reveal the navy blue, deep v tank top beneath. My heels click against the tile floors as I move closer to the tub, perching on the edge once more.

"I need someone that can think on their feet. You've survived the shit you get yourself into for this long," I start.

His eyes slowly open. They roll over me lazily, lust evident when he lingers on my breasts. I reach to lift his chin, bringing his eyes level with mine.

"You sure do like touching me," he grins.

"Listen to me," I snap. "The world knows me as Havana Bullock. Anita Harris was killed in a car accident the night I left that trailer park you grew up in. My father raised me and my brothers to be professional hitters.

"Augustine wasn't my biological father. He found us all and took us under his wing. Until two months ago, I would've thought my father loved me. He was good to me. Someone killed my father in his office.

"After we buried him, a video was sent to me from his lawyer. Dear old dad fucked me over. He had my accounts frozen and black balled me from the hitters' circuit. I'm left with bullshit jobs like your contract. Ten grand isn't even one percent of what I make on a hit.

"I'm out of money and nearly out of time. My father's stipulations said I had to find a husband and stay married for at least a year," I pause, letting the bitter taste of betrayal roll within my mouth. "During that time, my husband and I have to also have a baby. And I can't kill a soul. If I drop even one body during my first year of marriage I lose everything."

"The fuck?" he grunts at me. "First, I can't believe you're pouting because you can't kill anyone. Second, you ain't said shit over the phone about a baby."

"You wouldn't have come," I huff. "I need you to fit into my life Dallas. I need someone I can trust with my secrets and I need that baby."

"No," he shakes his head.

"What? Why the hell not?" I snarl.

"As much as I'd love to fuck you, I ain't shit and I know it. I'm not bringing a kid into this world to grow up to be a fuck up like me. No!" he barks.

"I don't have any more money. If we don't do this, I can't pay your debt and they will kill you. Once we're married the first fifteen million will be released. I can pay your debt and hold things together around here for a bit longer."

I hate the desperation I hear in my own voice. I sound lost, like the little girl that lost everything at age nine. Everything changed for me that night.

Augustine used to say that night was my destiny. I was born for him to find me. I'm the best out of the bunch. He took me under his wing and treated me just like I was his very own daughter.

"I wish I could help you, darlin', but I'm not your guy. Just look at the shit I got myself into," he says gently.

I don't want his sympathy. What I need is a husband, a baby, and to refrain from killing anyone for the first year of my marriage. My mind races as I mentally run the list of potential husband's again.

My jaw clenches. I can't stand weak men. If it's for a quick rump in the sack I can ignore certain things. I cannot blend a weak sniveling man into my life for an entire year. I just cannot.

Dallas is a lot of things but nothing I've learned about him in the last week and a half says he's weak. Before his latest problem, he'd been working his way towards a goal. I smile inside when that thought comes to me. I know things, things that will allow me to appeal to the heart of this man.

I retrieve my phone from my pocket, pulling up the pictures I need. I had a feeling this would be a bargaining chip. I need to build rapport with this man and I have the key right in my hand.

"I know you didn't get yourself into this mess. Congratulations, by the way," I say.

His eyes narrow on me. He searches my face for a clue as to what I'm talking about. When he doesn't find an answer, his lip curls up in a snarl.

"What are you talking about? I ain't got shit to be celebrating," he rumbles.

"Yes, you do. Your grades were great even for a drunk going to class online," I grin.

"How do you—" his mouth drops open, but clamps shut as a hard expression takes over his face.

"She really fucked you over, didn't she?" I say.

"What do you think you know?"

"You took that package from Skull to pay off the last of your school debt so you could get your degree. Payoff school, have a little something extra to get a nice suit to go on the job interviews you were lining up.

"It was all right there. So close you could taste it. Then, she snatched it all away. Ran off with the package and left you with more debt than your ass could cash. You tried. You got Skull as much as you could but with the interest he's been adding daily and the initial loss being nearly three hundred grand you've been drowning.

"Petty crimes that aren't your style. Becoming an accessory to a murder, robbing banks. You're in over your head, Dallas. You're a simple guy. This shit is eating you alive," I lean forward towards him.

"Which is exactly why I'm not getting mixed up with you or any other woman," he hisses.

"What if I told you I did you a little favor? I brought you a little gift," I purr.

27

He gives me a side glare. I lift my phone turning it towards him. He drops his cuffed hands in front of him leaning forward to squint at my photo. The color drains from his face.

"Is that…" his eyes bounce between the phone and my face. I nod.

"I don't like thieves. Especially, those that rob good people of their chance to better themselves."

His eyes lock on my face. He's silent as he stares back at me. I wait. I know what I did to his ex was sick and sadistic. Chopping off her thieving hands was the least of the shit I did to her. She pissed me off. She had no remorse for the situation she left Dallas in. Not even after I told her about the shit he's had to live through.

For the first time, he had something to hope for and be proud of. She took that from him. The filthy mess sitting before me is not Dallas. He'd become this after giving up hope. I can restore that hope if he'll help me.

"What if there's no baby?" he grumbles quietly.

"The other two hundred and fifty million disappears. Help me, I'll give you five million after the year instead of two," I lift a brow.

"Why tell me that you stand to lose two hundred and fifty million, but only offer me five? Ain't you worried about me asking for more or trying to take you for more than half?" his brows draw together and his eyes fill with curiosity.

I tilt my head and watch him. The boy I knew is still in there. I can see it. I may be a different person. Anita has been stripped away. She'll never come back, but Dallas is still Dallas.

I reach out to comb his damp hair to the side, the way I remember it as a little boy. He captures my wrist again, but with none of the force from before.

"Do you remember me?" I ask softly.

"Yeah," he grunts and nods.

"I remember you. It's weird because you're my only memories from back then. I don't remember my family or anything else from before the accident.

"But I've always remembered the little boy that was my best friend. I remember...you always let me eat most of the ice cream. We couldn't afford two cones. We had to share one every time. You never failed to let me have more, including letting me finish the cone.

"You're smart enough to make a life with five million. You wouldn't ask for more. It's why I chose you. You're one of the few people in my life that never betrayed me," I clamp my mouth shut, pulling my hand back and clearing my throat.

I reach into the water for the sponge floating on the surface. My eyes widen when I feel my fingers brush his length. My cheeks warm.

"I'm not promising you anything I can't give," he rasps. "I...I don't know if I can help you. Do I have time to think about this? Does Skull know I'm here?"

No and no.

I want to tell him that we're out of time. I need to free up those funds yesterday. Skull doesn't know I have him, but after tomorrow, I have a week and a half to send proof that I settled the mark. We could both be dead after that.

"We don't have long. I need to settle with Skull one way or the other by Friday after next," I reply.

"Alright," he frowns. "I'll answer by Friday."

Fuck!

"Fine," I murmur.

I reach for the soap to squeeze into the sponge and start to bath his shoulders. He's stiff as a board at first but soon begins to relax. When I finish with his body, I squeeze the shampoo into my palms and start to massage it into his hair.

"I should charge you another million for the free feels," he groans as I scratch his scalp.

"Can't trust my brothers not to kill you and I can't afford you running on me. You'll be sleeping with me until I know we're in this together. I don't want bedbugs or lice in my bed," I taunt.

"Fuck you," he mutters sounding hurt.

"Maybe, if this dirt washes off," I say with a smile in my voice.

His eyes lift to mine. I see the heat and lust there. Maybe playing with this man isn't such a good idea. I'll have to uncuff him sooner or later.

CHAPTER FOUR

What I do

Havana

It's been two days and Dallas hasn't given me an answer. The stress and tension has mounted to a point of choking me. Between the sexual tension between us and the unknown factor of my future, I needed to get out of the house.

I was grateful for the little hit that dropped into my lap. This guy I'd kill happily. He's been beating his wife within an inch of her life on a regular and has started in on the kids.

His mother in law saved up her money and pulled some from her pension to put out this hit. I'd have done it for free, if I didn't need the money. I already decided that if Dallas agrees to help me, I'll be dropping a package on her doorstep in the form of a refund.

This mark was easy to get close to. He nearly jumped my bones in the bar I so happened to run into him at. I didn't have to suggest going to my place twice.

Once in the parking lot his hands were all over me. In the locks of my lace front, gripping my ass. Not the actions of a devoted husband and loving father.

I giggled like an airhead while whispering dirty things in his ear. It was what I needed for him to change his mind from wanting a quickie in the parking lot. Instead, he opted to get in my car in hopes of a real deal night of the best sex of his life.

I'm sure he's regretting that car ride now, with both eyes swollen shut as he hangs upside down in my version of a playroom. I always love watching their faces when they think I'm into some kinky shit and they're about to get dominated. They make my job easy, practically tossing their own asses into my restraints and contraptions.

They never take note of the plastic lining the floor or the knife display along the wall on the far side of the room. They always say to be careful what you wish for. I only come here when I want to drag a hit out.

This was one I wanted to drag out as long as I could. I wanted him to feel the searing pain his wife has felt each of the four times he's broken her collarbone. Not to mention the ten wrist fractures, a broken nose and countless busted lips.

"How does it feel," I growl at him as I hold the pliers with another of his bloody teeth in my hand. "You like beating on helpless women and children? How does it feel to be the helpless one?"

"P…pl…please," he pleads through a mouth full of blood.

I move to the table, tossing the last of his teeth down along with the pliers, I reach for the tape. I turn back for his beaten body, squatting before him. I peel a piece of tape away, allowing him to see the roll in my hand.

"At this moment, all of your blood and fluids are rushing to your lungs and brain. All of those girly little martinis you were sucking down are going to fill your lungs," I purr, ripping off a piece of tape.

I slap it across his mouth, shutting up his whimpers. He pisses himself, pulling a hiss of disgust from me. I stand and move to sit in the chair I placed across from him. I stare into his eyes and watch the panic in them. Eventually, the life will start to drain from them nice and slow.

"We'll be here for a while," I croon.

His face is beet red, graduating to a shade of purple. His eyes are yellow and red, bulging. Tears soak his skin, rolling into his hairline.

I take out my phone and open my kindle app. I flip through my to be read list and find the book I've been meaning to read. I make myself comfortable and start reading. I feel the tension leave my body with each page, each minute, each hour.

I make it through three books before I get to watch the light drain from this piece of shit's eyes. I look up just in time to see it happen. A smile spreads across my face.

"All in a day's work."

CHAPTER FIVE

Keep Cover

Havana

"Stop fidgeting," I snap at Dallas.

"You put me in this monkey suit," he growls pulling at the collar of his dress shirt.

I try not to laugh. He's been whining like a baby since we left the house. Sad part is, if he would stop fidgeting, he looks fine as hell. Dallas cleans up nicely. The difference is like night and day. If I didn't know better I would certainly think that my date tonight was an above board real estate mogul—just like myself, if you ask the right people.

"Blue or brown?"

"What? Blue, I guess. What kind of question is that?" He grumbles.

I dig into my bag, pulling out the contact lens case. I hold it out to him. Dallas looks at it curiously.

"The blue contact is in the right side. Put it in. Tonight, you're Dallas Steel. No one here needs to know the name Echoes," I say.

"I never use that name," he grunts.

"Exactly. I don't know why and this isn't share time," I say pointedly. "We need to make you blend into this world. In this circle, I run a multi-million dollar real estate company. You are now a part of that. You've just relocated and you're bringing your experience to my team."

I inform him. I need him to fit in seamlessly. I plan to steer this night just as I need it.

"If you have this company, why not take the money from there?" he inquires.

"Lower your voice," I hiss.

"Well?" he whispers back.

"Because I've taken all I can without it becoming a problem. I touch one more dime and I'll bring hell down on everyone's head. I need you tonight, Dallas. This party is important. Appearances need to look just so," I whisper harshly.

He's silent as he looks over my face. I hate when he does that. He's been doing it since he woke in my tub. Whenever I don't tell him everything, he looks for the parts I'm leaving out. I feel bare each time he does it.

"You have the weight of the world on your shoulders, kitten," he grumbles in a low deep voice.

"You wouldn't understand," I turn away.

"Try me," he places a finger under my chin, turning my face back towards him.

"We're here," I say as the car stops.

I hand him a compact to use to get the contact in. I feel a ping in my chest when he slips the little lens in place. I prefer him without it, but tonight we need to recreate the man before me.

I move to slide out of the car, but Dallas's hand on my shoulder stops me. I turn to look back at him. He gives me that gorgeous smile, causing me to involuntarily squeeze my thighs together.

"You said I need to blend in," he murmurs.

He shifts to climb out of the limo before me. His large hand reaches back into the car for mine. I wrap my fingers around his and climb out.

Dallas looks down at me and winks. I can't help the shock that covers my face. His smile turns up a few notches.

"You remember old lady Parish?"

My brows knit. I shake my head at him. He reaches up to tuck a strand of hair behind my ear.

"She was the nice lady next door. We would go to her house for cookies. She would have us sit for tea, even taught us to dance together. Always said I could be a gentleman no matter where I came from," he says fondly of the memory.

"I looked after her until she passed a few years back. We continued to have tea and she continued to try to make a gentleman out of me. Never had use for any of it until now."

"You're just full of surprises, aren't you?" I smile back.

He leans into my ear, pausing for a beat.

"You have no idea, kitten," he croons.

"Watch it, Dallas. I have claws," I warn.

"Trust me, I know," he chuckles, wrapping an arm around my waist.

~B~

Dallas

I've been collecting questions in my head. I'm watching her. She has more secrets than one little kitten should hold alone. I can see the weight that's placed on her. She's hurting, which leaves her in a position to hurt others.

The trust she has in me floors me. She may not remember the past but she remembers us. She remembers who I once was. I don't know if she's so right about giving her trust to me now, but I want her to be.

I see it when she lets it slip through. The look in her eyes that makes me feel like someone else. It's like being a kid again, when she made me feel like somebody. She sees something in me others don't see.

It doesn't mean I don't think this is all crazy. Marriage and a kid? I don't think I can sign up for that, but what choice do I have? I'm stalling but my options aren't too great outside of her offer.

Yet, looking around this room of shirts. I don't know how long I can pull this off. I take a sip of the scotch in my hand. Anita's musical laugh pulls my attention. I turn to look at her a few feet away rubbing elbows with the wealthy. This is a long way from sharing ice cream cones in the trailer park.

"She's beautiful, isn't she?"

I turn to my right to see a brown skin guy staring at Anita. He's a few inches shorter than me, with caramel colored skin. His hazel eyes remain locked on Anita, sending a bolt of jealousy through me.

"Been trying to get her to settle down for years," he says turning his eyes towards me. "Now, I'm hearing talk of you being her new boyfriend."

"Fiancé," I say possessively.

His eyes fill with hurt and surprise. Oh, little Anita, you were fucking this one. That knowledge burns my chest. I don't like it one bit.

"She's never dated. Not a committed relationship," he says, his words tinged with disbelief.

"When it's right, it's right," I shrug taking another sip of my drink.

"Where did you two meet?"

"Ross," Anita interrupts as she slips up to my side.

I place an arm around her waist. A smile tugs at my lips when she turns into my embrace, placing a hand on my chest. Ross looks like someone just drove a stake through his heart.

"Havana, you're looking as gorgeous as ever. I guess I see why you haven't called me in a while," he replies.

"I was grieving," she says tightly. "I told you I needed time."

"And yet, here you are engaged," he says bitterly.

I notice the slight twitch of surprise in her eyes. She hadn't introduced me as more than her boyfriend this evening. However, something about this guy made me say more.

"Well, then, that makes two of us. Doesn't it?" she tosses back.

"That's low. I explained that situation to you," he says tightly.

"Only after hiding the fact for how long?" she tilts her head.

"Doesn't matter now, does it?" I interject.

"Sure doesn't," she replies.

"Honey, I have some friends that want to meet you," she turns that bright smile up at me.

"Of course," I say dipping my head to kiss her cheek.

Her lashes lower shyly and it throws me back in time. She was definitely a shy little girl. I remember it clearly.

We walk off with Ross forgotten. I'm now captivated by the glow in her cheeks. When she looks up at me through her lashes, something tugs in my chest.

"You're doing great by the way," she whispers up at me.

"Told you not to doubt me," I wink.

"We make the perfect couple," she says with a little grin.

"Now, you might be going too far. I've seen the way men look at you. You have several options better suited for you," I grumble.

"*Now* who's underestimating you?"

"Stating facts," I shrug.

"Looks can be deceiving. Point out one of the men here that you think would be a better choice than you and I can reveal that you're sorely mistaken," she retorts.

I look around the room. I don't want to point out the men I've wanted to punch throughout the night, but my curiosity has gotten the best of me. I want to know what I have that in her mind these millionaires don't.

"Him," I nod at the blonde that would have sold his right kidney to get me out of the way earlier just so he could claim all of her attention.

"Ah, Brock Rushing. His net worth is an estimated hundred sixty million. He's part owner of an alternative energy developmental firm in New Castle. He also makes women disappear, literally," she turns her face up to see my reaction.

"What?"

"Trafficking. He dates them, ties them up and has his way, then sells them to the highest bidder. All after it's streamed live for the duration of their captivity," I reply.

"You can't be serious?"

"Very. He doesn't discriminate either. If you're in this circle and you're dumb enough to follow him home, you asked for it.

"Look over there. Payton Crisco, notice the way he's been glaring at Brock. A few months back Payton's loving fiancée was seen leaving out of the backdoor with Brock. No one has seen her since."

"You're kidding?"

She shrugs.

"Pick someone else," she says.

I look around again. I stop on a dark haired guy that's currently devouring my date with his eyes. You would think he had x-ray vision. I nod toward him.

"Stevie," she giggles. "First of all, he's bi-sexual. Which hey, do your thing. The problem is he likes to date in triangles. That's not for me. Secondly, while he would have everyone in this room to believe he is worth five hundred million, it hasn't been so since his father's death.

"Asshole gambled half of his fortune away in the first six months. He's here looking for his next sucker to milk," she snorts.

"How do you know all of this?"

"It's my job to know all of this," she replies.

"Why the cover, when these guys sound as shady as you are?"

Fuck. I didn't mean for it to come out like that.

She turns to give me a sharp look. Her eyes scan my face. A flicker of hurt flashes in her gaze for all but a second.

"You think I'm shady?"

"That's not what I meant—"

"It is," she cuts me off. "It's your opinion. You don't know or understand me. These men are in a league of their own. They all feel entitled to the debauchery they inflict on the world.

40

"Their money gives them power that no man should have a right to. They also grant me the access to hide in plain sight. This is the nucleus of information in this room. If you want to know anything about the rich and famous, these men and women will reveal it.

"My team provides them with a service. We find them houses, secret getaways, luxury to put up a front if necessary. In return, they all want to be Havana's friend, sharing their deepest secrets with me.

"I've never sold a single house. That's what Aisha, my assistant does. But everyone in this room wants to be a part of something great and Augustine sold them an illusion. He and I were the best of the best, even if we'd never shown a single property face to face.

"You think I'm shady, but I'm the cleanest one in this room. If they knew the truth, it would put me and everyone I care about in danger. The pawns would revolt. Do you understand now?"

She eyes me searchingly. Again she has placed trust in me. I have gathered enough information in my time with her to pull the pins that hold her life together. If I go through with this and she comes into her inheritance, I could ruin her and make off with it all.

"Dallas, you're not that crazy and you're not stupid. Crossing me would end very badly for you. I tell you things because I trust you, but I'd kill you if this one time in my life I happened to misjudge a person," she says as if reading my thoughts, before turning to sashay away.

I watch as her hips sway. She's one dangerous woman. In mind and body. I still think these people are innocent next to her. She'd just burn them all down in one of these parties if they turned on her.

CHAPTER SIX

Trouble

Havana

I haven't been able to sleep. While Dallas did amazing the other night at the gala, we still have a problem brewing. I'm almost out of time.

I should never have taken the job. If I don't settle Dallas's debt or prove that he's no longer breathing, I'm next. I don't even have the protection of the circle, thanks to my dear old dad. They'll come after me too for taking an outside job to begin with.

Dallas needs to make a decision. There's no more time or money. The last two properties Aisha moved into escrow funded me paying the boys. I claimed it was money owed from past jobs.

I can't keep lying to my brothers. They're suspicious as it is. I can see it in their eyes. They don't like Dallas. They don't understand what I want with him and that's making them all twitchy, especially Will.

Will and I have been a part of the family the longest. Augustine brought him home not too long after he found me. He's the most protective of me.

I can't have them asking questions. They're a bunch of hot heads. If I told them we stand to lose everything, it's no telling what they'd all get themselves into.

What I haven't told Dallas is that my inheritance isn't the only one on the line. Every dime we've ever earned as individual hitters has always been looked after and held in accounts by Augustine.

All of that now hangs in the balance. He froze my access to those accounts, keeping me from being able to continue to pay out allowances. For years, we never questioned him controlling our accounts and giving us an allowance to live by. He never limited what we wanted to spend if we asked for more than the monthly stipend, therefore we'd never questioned him.

The ten of us trusted his loyalty without question when we never should have. He shitted on us. Leaving three of us on the short end of the equation and placing my back against the wall. I don't understand it.

Augustine only left seven of us all of his money to split. The other three will only walk away with what they earned. If, and only if, I follow through with his demands from the grave. We all blindly trusted him and it's biting me in my behind.

I always knew there were seven of us that Augustine truly favored as his children. I just didn't expect him to leave the others out the way he has. It's just one of the reasons I haven't told the others what's going on.

This will hurt some feelings, but if I don't play by the rules we all lose everything. I'm under enough pressure without telling the boys. I don't need them breathing down my neck to just pick someone to get married so we're not all in the poor house.

"Stop shaking," Dallas's husky voice fills the room as his warm palm settles on my thigh.

I hadn't noticed I'd been swaying my bent leg back and forth as I stared up at the ceiling. It's an old nervous habit. The motion calms me down.

However, now that my leg has stopped, tension coils within my body and it has nothing to do with my thoughts. Dallas's warm, rough hand sends currents rocking through my body. My core begins to come to life from the simple touch.

I've surprisingly gotten used to having him in my bed. The first three nights I kept him hand cuffed. After that I started to lock the bedroom door against the outside and I placed a sensor on the inside to alert me if my guest tried to leave.

His hand starts to slide higher up my thigh and my breath catches. The trail of fire he's leaving on my skin has my nipples tightening. It's been awhile, but I'm sure even if it hadn't been, Dallas's caress would cause me to toss out all caution and good sense.

His hand gets all the way up to my inner thigh before I realize the shift in density of its weight. It's not a gentle caress any longer. His hand has become pure dead weight. Next comes the sound of his snores.

"Really?" I huff.

I fold my arms over my chest and pout. Now I'm horny and frustrated. I have too much on my mind and his hand now at the apex of my thighs has me throbbing in places I've been just fine ignoring.

Seconds tick by, as I wait to see if he's just pulling my leg. It's only wishful thinking. The man is knocked out. I start to debate whether or not to put the fire out on my own.

What the hell. It'll let off some of this stress.

I reach down, slipping my hand into my silk pajama shorts. I'm no stranger to making this happen for myself. Starting a slow circular motion around my nub, I get my juices to really flow. As my fingertips become moist, I reach with my free hand to pinch my nipple.

The heat of his hand resting on me heightens the sparks that shoot through me. I slip my fingers into my wetness and start to pump. I bite my lip to keep from moaning aloud. My head sinks back into the pillow.

This is just what I needed. It's been much too long since I gave this part of my body attention. I close my eyes as my breathing becomes labored. My hips begin to rock, causing his fingers to flex against me.

My eyes flash open and I still. I find one blue eye, one hazel staring back at me. It's clear that he's awake now. His nostrils flare as lust fills his gaze. He licks his lips, his eyes dropping to the hand I still have shoved into my shorts.

"Need some help," he rasps, his voice thick with lust.

I open my mouth to say yes, but something catches my attention. Lightning fast, I reach for my gun beneath the pillow. My wet core is forgotten as I aim and shoot pass Dallas's head.

His eyes go wide. I push him aside and fire a few more rounds into the darkness. The distinct sound of bodies dropping can be heard. I hop from the bed moving to clear the room before turning on the lights.

There are three bodies lying in my bedroom. I suck my teeth and stomp my foot. They're totally going to mess up my carpet. The white fibers are already starting to soak up the blood.

"How—how the hell did they get in here? I watched you lock the door and set the sensor," Dallas says in confusion as he stares down at the bodies.

"Do you know them?" I stoop down by the one nearest my feet.

He looks familiar, even with a bullet in his forehead. When I look to my right at one of the others, I know exactly where I know the first one from. They were the ones that brought me the request for the job on Dallas.

"Nicky, Harp, and Mick, they're Skulls guys," he replies as he moves to stand over me. "Are you okay?"

"Yeah, but this shit is ruining my carpet," I huff.

I run a hand over my scarfed head. This has just turned into a mess. Skull isn't just going to go away. I have questions.

"How did they get in?" he repeats.

They were here all along. They had to have come in while we were out. I stand and turn to look over at my bathroom. Both walk-ins are big enough to hide in and not be found. As Dallas doesn't have much use for the closet they were surely able to stow away inside that one.

All they had to do was wait and then creep through the bathroom into the bedroom. They weren't on the other side of the locked door. Now, my question is, why did Skull send them?

I still have time on my contract. Also, how did they know so much about my set up? Something smells fishy. My internal radar is going off.

"Talk to me, Anita. Who other than your goons that brought me here know about me or that I'm here?" his words burst through my thoughts. "Could anyone at that party have told Skull they saw me with you?"

"No. Our world isn't the type of shit they want a view into. Augustine handled things for them when they needed on a don't ask, don't tell policy. They didn't know how he did it or if he was the one to do it. No blood on the sheets, no crime to trace back to their door steps."

"Someone had to tell Skull something. Why would they come here?" Dallas tugs at his hair.

"Don't you think I know this," I hiss in frustration.

"Who knows I've been here with you?"

"Aisha," I reply.

"Is that it?"

"My brothers," I answer trying to catch up to my nagging thoughts.

"The three assholes that brought me here?"

"Yes, no," I shake my head trying to think. "I have five others. It's possible they know."

"Could one of them hav—,"

"Enough," I snap. I can't think with him talking.

My first instinct is to get the hell out of here. He's right. Someone has been talking and we're not safe here. I also get the feeling something more is going on, but we can't stay here to find out what.

"Get dressed. Take only what you need that can fit on your person," I command and head for my closet to get dressed.

Augustine's voice plays loudly in my head, creating a stone of dread in the pit of my stomach. He'd always said I was too trusting as a child. It was the one thing he felt was a flaw when it came to me becoming the perfect assassin.

'Trust no one, Havana. As an assassin you will never be able to trust a soul. Even those closest to you are a threat because they can only be trusted as far as the value of their own trust,' he had said. 'Do you really want to place your life in the hands of someone else's trust?'

I don't think I ever fully understood his words, but something tells me that I'm about to learn their meaning first hand. Only nine other living people know how to get into my home. There's no way those three were able to get in here undetected without help.

When I find out who helped them, I'm going to kill them. I close my eyes and drop my head. Where am I going to go? I'm out of money and even if somehow I talked Dallas into helping me, I can't kill anyone for a year.

I'm so fucked. I place my palms to the shelves in front of me. I stiffen when arms circle my waist. I know it's Dallas, I've learned his scent.

"It seems we're in this together now. I'll do it. We can't run without money. So I'll do it. Something ain't right around here, kitten. I may not be the brightest bulb in the shed, but I know a coup when I see one," he says in my ear.

I turn around in his arms and look up at him sharply.

"Stop saying things like that. You're not stupid. If we're going to do this…. Just know I chose you for a reason. You're smart and you know how to adapt," I force out.

He studies me with those eyes, unnerving me as usual. Not ready for him to see my thoughts, I knock his hands away. I step around him to continue to get ready.

I already have on a pair of leather pants and a black t-shirt. I shove my feet into a pair of black ankle boots and snatch a leather jacket. I move quickly out of the closet to exit the bedroom.

I need to get to my office. Once there, I grab my backpack and make my way into my saferoom. I toss a few passports, guns, and the last five grand I put aside in case something like this happened. It's not much and won't get us far, but it's what I have.

Movement on the monitors in my safe room catches my attention. I narrow my eyes on the screen. I don't know what to make of the sight of all my brothers making their way to my front door.

What are they doing here?

They seem to be arguing, but I don't have time to sit and analyze this. The hairs on the back of my neck stand up. I'm going to go with my gut and my gut is telling me to take Dallas and get the fuck out of here.

"Let's go," I bark and head out the office French doors that lead outside to the backyard.

We creep around to the garage. Dallas rushes for the car, but I reach for his arm and shake my head. I nod towards my bike.

"We'll cover more ground on it," I whisper.

He twists his lips, looking as if he wants to protest, but he nods. I go to hop on, only to have his arm snake around my waist. I look up at him curiously.

"I'll drive," he murmurs. "Don't argue. We don't have time."

I grind my teeth, but I do as he says. As he straddles the bike, I run to punch the button for the garage door, cursing it's loud sound as it opens. I rush back over, jumping on behind him, wrapping my arms around his waist. Dallas walks the bike out of the garage with me clinging to him and the engine still off.

"Hey, Havana," I hear called in the not too far distance.

"Let's go," I growl.

The bike comes to life beneath us and Dallas guns us down the driveway and out of the gate. I look behind us to see Will running after us. My heart squeezes in my chest. They were my family, my brothers. I can't wrap my head around them wanting me dead.

CHAPTER SEVEN

I'll do it

Dallas

She's exhausted. I can see it in her face. We only stopped for gas, but we'll need to get a room somewhere soon or she's likely to slide right off the back of the bike.

I need to recharge myself. The adrenaline is starting to wear off and my brain is running in so many directions.

"Kitten, we need to find some place to rest up," I say as I watch her lids droop.

"No, we have to keep moving. I'll drive if you're tired," she shakes her head, a frown on her pretty face.

"You ain't driving me no place like that," I point at her sleepy eyes. "You need some sleep."

"No."

"Listen—"

"No, you listen. I'm one of ten of the best trained assassins out there. There's a chance that the other ten are now after my life. If they're trying to find me, we need to keep moving," she barks.

I clamp my mouth shut, my own temper threatening to boil over. The thought of those cowards coming for her life leaves a real bad taste in my mouth. I watch her, but I don't say another word as I finish pumping the gas.

"We have to keep moving until I can figure out where we can get some more money. I need resources and some place safe to think," she mumbles to herself.

"Wait a minute," I grunt. "You said we'd have access to fifteen million once we marry."

"We're not married. I can't get my hands on that money until I have a husband," she groans, reaching to rub her temples.

I replace the nozzle into the pump and twist the cap back onto the bike. I move to lift her chin, catching her tired eyes. She looks back at me warily.

"I said I'll do it. I meant it. Let's get married and get us some money," I smile at her.

I see the hesitation in her eyes. I pull my hand back from her face. I should have known she'd come to her senses sooner or later. No matter how much she's cleaned me up, I'm still me.

"Once we're married, I can't kill anybody for a year," she pouts.

I stare at her. I mean really stare at her. I can see that her words are the honest point of her reluctance. Here I am thinking she's having second thoughts about me and lo and behold she's thinking about not killing anyone for a year.

"Then, I guess we better disappear once we get that money so you don't have to," I give her a lopsided grin.

CHAPTER EIGHT

The Wedding

Havana

"What am I doing," I huff to myself.

I've never been that girl. You know, the type to daydream about her wedding, picking bridesmaids, color schemes, and wishing for the perfect groom. I never thought I'd see the day when I'd walk down the aisle.

This feels so odd. My heart is pounding as I move towards Dallas, the man I'm about to marry. It was his idea to do it this way, since we have to send proof to Augustine's lawyers. Not just a certificate, but photos and/or video.

We took the little money I had and purchased two tickets to St. Croix. The beautiful water and skies will provide a picture perfect wedding. We had just enough to pay for my simple white sundress, Dallas's white linen suit, gold bands, the license, a photographer, and a room for the next two nights.

We won't be able to stay here long. We had to marry under our legal names, which will leave a paper trail. As soon as that money hits my offshore account, we're going to have to relocate and make Havana and Dallas Echoes disappear.

Dallas talked a local kid into recording with my phone for a few bucks. The feed is live. It's streaming directly to the lawyer on facetime. I'm hoping that will get his ass in gear to release that money.

"You look beautiful," Dallas murmurs when I stop before him.

"Thank you," I reply, lowering my lashes.

"Come on, Rev. Let's get me married before she changes her mind," Dallas chuckles.

I look up to see him watching me with mirth in his eyes. I can also see nervousness. Not for the first time, I feel sorry for dragging him into this. I still plan to settle that debt for him. Skull will have what's owed him. Now, if he still wants to come for us, that's his funeral. A year doesn't last forever.

~B~

Dallas

I'm married. I keep repeating it in my head, waiting for it to become reality. The relief I see in my wife's face is well worth it. It's the most relaxed I've ever seen her.

Sure enough, as soon as we said I do, the money was wired to her account. We already have a flight booked off of this island in the morning. We decided not to stay the two nights.

We'll pay out the reservation to make it look like we're here, but Anita and Norris will be on that plane headed to Columbia. No one knows the name I knew her by as a kid. Norris was the name on the passport Anita had shoved in her bag with my face on it.

I don't know if I should be alarmed or impressed that she was prepared with documents with my face already on them. Her thinking ahead will make moving around a hell of a lot easier.

"Why do you keep looking at me like that," she says softly, while looking up at me through her lashes.

"I can't stop thinking about that kiss," I reply.

I hadn't planned to do more than peck her lips for the camera after we said I do. However, the moment my lips touched hers, sparks flew and I couldn't help devouring her sweet mouth. It took everything in me to pull away and not mull her right there on the beach.

"Um, hey, that was something," she breathes, her eyes falling on my lips.

I take a pull of my beer. We've been drinking in the little outdoor bar for the best part of the last two hours. A little wedding celebration of sorts.

"I look forward to a repeat," I say after swallowing.

"I've been Mrs. Steel for almost five hours now and my husband has only kissed me once. Either I did something very wrong the first time or I'm not his type," she says with a little sexy grin on her lips.

I place my beer on the bar top, reaching for her with my other hand. Cupping her face with my now free hand, I tilt her head up. When I capture her lips, I feel that zing of electricity that zips through me.

Her flavor is robust. Like aged whiskey that rolls down the throat smoothly and warms the belly. I want to drink from her lips until I'm drunk off of her essence.

I pull her closer, until she's standing between my legs, chest to chest with me. Her arms go around my neck, clinging to me like a man worthy of a woman like her. I feel like my heart is going to explode out of my chest if I don't have more of her.

My hands slide down to her ass and begin to knead her lush curves. I have two hands full of her globes and it feels damn good.

"We should go to our room," she purrs into my mouth.

"Only if you plan to play with your pussy for me. I never did get to finish watching that show," I rasp back.

"Careful what you ask for. You may get more than you bargain for," she replies.

"I think we still have a part of this arrangement to fulfill," I remind her. "I'm clean. If you want to wait to find out."

"I have the results to your last examination a month ago," she says sheepishly.

"I'm starting to feel at a disadvantage. You're going to start filling in some of the gaps to level the playing field," I grumble.

"Stop pouting," she chuckles. "Let's go. I'm dripping down my thighs from that kiss."

"Damn," I growl, squeezing her ass in my palms.

CHAPTER NINE

Mr. and Mrs.

Havana

Dallas has me wrapped around his waist the moment we walk into the room. The man kisses like he can taste my soul through my lips. His tongue leaves no surface in my mouth untouched.

I love the way his hands search my body in a possessive way. As if every curve belongs to him. It's intoxicating. He nips at my chin, then licks from the base of my throat back to his starting point.

I shiver in his hold. My back hits the wall beside the door. He reaches for the straps of my dress, pulling them down my shoulders and arms. Goosebumps cover my skin as his fingertips graze my flesh.

"Dallas," I sigh.

"Keep calling my name like that we're going to have a problem," he rasps.

"Dallas," I say again, challenging him.

He hisses, pushing my dress the rest of the way off my body. He pins me to the wall as he lowers to hook my legs over his shoulders. I claw at the wall behind me as he lifts me up it. His mouth covers my sex through my panties.

I forget finding purchase behind me, locking my fingers in his hair. Dallas places one hand on the wall, while the other locks around my thigh. He sucks and licks at me until the fabric between his mouth and my center is just a wet scrap.

His tongue hooks into my panties, pushing them aside so he can reach the dripping lips awaiting him. He uses his face to gain the access he needs, like a skilled professional pussy eater. I ride his face for every red cent he's worth.

I look down to watch him, my mouth hanging open as my face twists in awe. His head bobs and rolls into my core like he's having the most passionate, intimate conversation of his life. His eyes are locked on me the entire time. The sight turns me on so much.

"Damn, you better eat that shit," I moan.

He groans into me, delivering on my demand. My head falls back against the surface behind me, my eyes rolling up towards the sky. I try to climb the wall to get away. It's too good.

"Play with it, Kitten," he pulls back to croon.

"Mm," I hum.

Reaching between my legs, I rock my hips against his face at the same time that I play with my clit. The orgasm that rocks me almost sends me jerking from his hold. Dallas tightens his grip and lowers me down the wall.

When his lips capture mine, my flavor assaults my mouth. I suck at his lips and tongue. I cup his face to hold him still while I clean his face of my essence.

I hear and feel as he frees himself of his pants, shoving them down his waist. He reaches to tear out the crotch of my panties. His thumb finds my nub, while two of his other fingers probe my center. He pumps those fingers in and out of me.

"Please," I plea.

"Been wanting you long enough. Time to put us both out of our misery," he grunts before aligning himself and driving home.

He stills and releases a loud groan. His cheeks redden, a vein pops in the side of his neck. My fingers tremble as I reach for his shoulders to steady myself. I've never been so full.

Dallas is reaching places that have never been touched. It's right on the edge of pain and pleasure. I bite my lip and look into his eyes.

His palms reach to squeeze my ass, starting to guide me up and down his length. We moan in unison, curses ripping from his lips. I clench around him and his head falls back.

Dallas sets a punishing pace, only to slow down for long drawn out tortuous strokes. If a man could talk with his dick, this man would have perfected the art. His eyes seem to punctuate each stroke with a message.

I watch his eyes as I feel him lay claim to my pussy. I have no question as to who's owning my body stroke for stroke, pound for pound. Trust, I know who's it is. The question is written on his face as he lifts a brow at me.

"Yes, Dallas," I cry.

"Damn, you're so wet," he grunts. "Pussy this tight is a sin, baby. I'm going to need a whole lot of saving after this."

He's one to talk. I'm sure I'm losing my sanity with each stroke of that fat beast between his legs. His fine ass has me drooling, literally. I reach to wipe the back of my hand across my mouth, but he stops me. Leaning in, he licks my face where the drool is running.

"Ain't never had pussy this good. You've got me doing stupid shit," he breathes against the corner of my mouth.

Burying his face into my neck he bites me. I yelp and come all over him. A rumbling sound comes from his chest. He pulls me from the wall. I cling to his shoulders as I convulse on his rod.

My back hits the bed with a bounce. He reaches behind me to release my bra. My breasts jiggle free. His head dips so that he can latch onto my nipple. My toes curl from the strong pulling and sucking he places on my peak.

He starts to rock inside of me again and I can feel the buildup roaring to life once more. I rock my hips with his, determined to ride it out with him. My breast pops free from his lips. He shifts to lift my legs to his shoulders, planting his palms on the mattress.

At this angle he starts to slide in deeper connecting with an entirely new spot. I can't help screaming my head off. It's so good. I reach for his hands, digging my nails into the top of his skin.

"Tell me what you like," he commands.

"I want you to hit it from the back and I don't mean my pussy," I pant.

~B~

Dallas

This woman is going to slay me. I've heard shit talking about black girls being less willing to take it in the ass. Of all of my white girl friends only two were brave enough to try me there.

Blue Saffire

Hearing Anita request me there has my balls so tight I think they might explode. I hate stereotypes. They'll keep you from some of the greatest experience of your life. This is one experience I'll never forget.

I've never had a pussy that sucked me in like a trap door with no release. The more I pound the more she squeezes and I can't get enough of it. I can feel the tingling in my toes.

As her words sink in, turning me on to the point of losing what mind I have left, I pull out. I get ready to flip her onto all fours, but she moves faster, knocking me back onto my heels. I watch as those sexy lips wrap around me.

I love a woman that enjoys the taste of her own cream. I watch as she sucks me dry, then soaks my cock all over again. A nasty girl after my own heart. My hips pump to assist her in her gifted snatching of my soul.

My hands grip the sheet as a low rumble rises from deep within my chest. I reach to massage her back as she works us both into a state of euphoria. Her enthusiasm for giving head is reward worthy.

I want to come, but not in her mouth. Reaching for her shoulders I interrupt the best blowjob of my life. Cupping her jaw, I meet her half way to take her lips. I kiss her hard, demanding more of her sweet mouth.

Breaking the kiss, I shift to reposition her on all fours. I dive at her ass, taking a bite. She moans and wiggles her cheeks in my face. I give one a hard slap.

"Dallas," she purrs my name in that sexy voice.

Spreading her cheeks for my view, I bite my lip shaking my head. What a beautiful sight. I dip to taste her again. She's so sweet and juicy. I lick her from front to back, lingering when I get to her puckered hole. I start to feast there preparing her to receive me.

"Please," she pleas.

"You'll get it soon enough," I chuckle.

I lift to shift behind her, sliding into that wet, tight, warm goodness again. My pelvis slaps against her lush round ass as I drill into her. It hits me that I'm fucking my wife.

The woman beneath me that's allowing me to have my way with her body—while enjoying the best sex of my life—is my wife. This gorgeous full figured, smart and lethal woman is mine. Maybe not in the conventional way, but at this point I don't give a shit. She belongs to me.

The need to claim and possess all of her fills me. My thumb becomes intrusive at her forbidden hole. I prime her for the real thing. My own breathing increasing with the anticipation of it all.

When I feel her come all over me once more, I know it's time to set claim to the only part of her I haven't been in. I pull out and align with her tight ring. I spit on my cock, rubbing the tip against her.

When I start to ease my way in, her sweet whimpers are like music to my ears. I want more, more of her, more of her cries for me. I don't know what I did to deserve her, but I have no idea how I'm ever supposed to give her up after this.

After a few easy, shallow strokes, I find myself seated to the hilt. My neck tenses and my toes dig into the bed. I bend my head to lick up her back and nip her shoulder. When I start to plow into her, we both go insane.

"Fuck," I hiss. "This ass. Damn, come for me. I'm not going to last."

"Harder, Dallas. I can handle it," she cries out.

I give her what she asks for and we both rocket across the finish line. I come so hard I feel it in my brain. I blink the spots away as I collapse over her.

"Now, that's how you consummate a marriage," she giggles.

"Damn, right," I murmur.

CHAPTER TEN

Remember Me

Dallas

"You were so tiny, but you were bossy even back then," I chuckle.

"Me, bossy?" she gasps. "You told me I was going to be your friend that first day."

"I was stating a fact. After you called those kids out for making fun of me, I knew we'd be friends," I shrug and begin to rub my hand up and down her back.

"I only told him the truth. How could he keep calling you dirty and stupid when he had on dirty holey clothes and he couldn't spell idiot? He had no right calling you one," she says of the memory.

"You were the only one to ever stand up for me," I muse.

"You were a sweet boy. You were the only one that would play with me without picking on me," she shrugs, turning her face up to look at me. "I guess we were a pair."

I search her eyes, getting lost in their depths. Her words strike a chord inside me. I've always gone through life feeling and thinking I was alone. I like the sound of being a pair with her.

I lift up to dip my head to capture her swollen lips. I don't think I'll get my fill of this woman. We've spent most of the night burning up these sheets and here I am hard as a rock wanting more of her.

"I want you, but we better get ready to catch our flight. We can sleep on the plane," I say against her lips.

She releases a loud groan, rolling off of my chest on to her back. I chuckle following her, instead of getting up to get ready. I can't help being close to her. I reach for her thigh, pulling it over my hip.

"You remember so much about us, but you don't remember your family or that night?" I ask the question that's been rattling in my brain.

"Yeah. Augustine said I hit my head pretty bad. I was lucky he found me when he did," she says.

"But you remember me?"

"Yeah, I don't know. I always had memories of you. I think it was a happy time for me. I started to remember more once I found out who you were," she replies thoughtfully.

"I'm glad you remembered me. I might be somewhere with a bullet in my head if you hadn't," I blurt out.

"You're debt is paid. You don't owe Skull a thing. I had the lawyer take care of it. Doesn't mean trouble isn't still coming for us. You're just square on what you owe," she informs me.

"Thanks," I nod.

She gives a warm smile. It lights up her pretty brown eyes and places a glow on her brown cheeks. I reach to run my thumb across her full lips, wishing I could bottle that smile to carry with me through my life.

I wouldn't dare dream that any of this will last past a year or the time it takes to get us out of danger. I'm still in awe of her allowing me inside of her. I feel like I've touched the edge of heaven and now they're coming for me to claim the price of my transgression.

"I paid off your student balance as well. When we get back, you'll have your degree waiting for you."

I focus in on her words and her eyes. I have to swallow down the lump in my throat. I worked so hard to get that degree. I'd been damn proud to make it to the end. When I was told I had to pay five thousand dollars before I could graduate and get my degree in hand, I felt like I was being laughed at for trying.

It was the beginning of it all being taken from me. I try to find the words to thank her, but they don't come. She'll never know what this means to me.

"You did the work. The money was a small thing compared to that," she says as if reading my thoughts.

I take her lips in a passionate kiss, allowing my tongue to say what my mind won't allow me to formulate into words. We'll get ready, it will just be in a little while. First, I need my wife to feel me.

CHAPTER ELEVEN

Answers

Havana

"Havana, where are you?" Aisha rushes into the phone.

"I can't tell you that. I don't know who I can trust. Did you get the money I sent?"

"Yes, but we're all worried about you," she says.

"I'm sure. I need answers. You're the only one I told about the money and what Augustine did. How do I know you didn't set this all up?" I accuse.

"You can't be serious," Aisha gasps. "I would never put you in danger. And there's something you should know. Will, Rich, Tristan, Bastian and Theo all already know. Apparently, Augustine made sure they knew as well.

"They've been waiting for you to tell them. I know there's more you're all not telling me, but I find it odd that they knew.

Why wouldn't Augustine tell me or the others?" Aisha's words are filled with hurt.

I believe her. Aisha wouldn't benefit from getting rid of me. Augustine made it clear that the others needed me to get the money. Aisha has as much to lose as the rest of us. If I die the money is gone. It was in the rules.

Which has my thoughts racing. If Will, Rich, Tristan, Bastian, and Theo know everything, then they would be fools to want me dead. Something isn't adding up.

"I need a favor. I need to know who let those guys into my house. I didn't have time to get my laptop. I need you to remote me into the system. I just sent you an encrypted email from a Yin Ling. Use it to get me in. I need to see who's logged as accessing my house that day," I say.

"Already on it," she replies.

"Also, see if you can find out who knew about Dallas other than the boys. See if they told anyone else. Why did Skull send his guys? I still had time to fulfill the contract. What made them come for me?"

"Havana, that's the other thing I was going to tell you. Will found Skull dead. It wasn't fresh. A day or two had passed by the time he found him. I don't think Skull sent those guys," Aisha says allowing her words to hang in the air.

"You be careful," I say quietly. "Trust no one."

"I'm already in the wind. My place was broken into the same night as your attack. I wasn't home, but I don't think they meant to leave me alive if I were," she says.

"Shit," I hiss. "Are you okay?"

"Yeah, I'm safe. I knew you would call so I've been watching this line making sure it stays secure."

"Have the boys been acting strange?"

She hesitates for the briefest moment, causing my hackles to go up. I narrow my eyes as if she's before me and I can see through her. Aisha is getting ready to lie to me. She hasn't told a lie yet, but she's about to.

This is the reason Augustine never thought she was ready for the job. She gives herself away. Aisha is perfect for an in and out long distance kill, but she sucks at engaging or wiggling her way out of tough spots. She's a terrible liar. Then, there's her other *little* problem.

"I haven't seen any of them since the day after the night you disappeared," she says softly.

"I have to go," I say and hang up.

I stare out the window at the ocean view at the back of the house. I picked this place for the access to the water as an escape and the lush trees that surround the front. The property is nice and tucked away.

But what am I tucked away from?

What's going on back home? What is Aisha hiding from me? What the hell has my father set in motion? More importantly, did we kill the right guy for his murder?

I'm getting the sense this is all connected and nine times out of ten, I'm right. I'm always right. I'm not naive enough not to start connecting this from the beginning. Something more is happening here. I just need to see the bigger picture.

I get to work as soon as I get remote access to my home computers and cameras. When I get into the logs, my head starts to hurt. Nothing makes sense. I don't even understand what I'm looking at. My mind reels.

It's impossible.

"What's up, Sunshine?" Dallas croons as he walks into the room.

I turn to glare at him. How do I know he doesn't have something to do with all of this? I feel like a caged animal. I don't know who I can trust.

"What's your problem?" he asks when I don't respond to him.

"I left you unattended for a few hours that day. What did you do while I was gone?"

"You have to be shitting me. You left me cuffed to your fucking bed," he hisses.

I purse my lips, turning back to my computer screen. Closing my eyes I rub my temples. He's right. I did cuff him. I needed to focus on something. I didn't have time to worry about him taking off or causing trouble.

"That means they had to get in after we left, which makes even less sense," I murmur to myself.

"You want to tell me what's going on," he bites out.

Turning toward him, I allow our eyes to lock. I curse my body for reacting to him. I fully take him in, causing my pulse to race and heat to spread to all the forbidden places.

He must have been out in the pool. His swim trunks are damp and his wet hair is falling into his eyes. He has in a single hazel contact, giving him two brown eyes.

His skin has been kissed by the sun deepening his olive tone. At the moment, he could easily pass for one of the beautiful Columbian men I've seen on this island. Or at least give them a run for their money.

His arms fold over his chest, causing his muscles to flex. I shake the lust away, lifting my eyes back to his gaze. He's waiting for an answer but I'm not sure I want to share. I don't even know what I'm sharing.

"Anita," he barks.

71

I lift a brow at him, crossing my own arms defiantly. He rolls his eyes, stepping forward to squat before me. His big hand comes up to cup my face.

"I ain't the enemy, kitten. You were hired to take my life, remember? Skull is after my ass as much as he's after yours. We're in this together," he says gruffly.

"Skull is dead," I say, watching for his reaction.

Surprise covers his face. His brows pinch in the center of his forehead. I can see the wheels turning within.

"One of your brothers?" he asks.

"I don't think so. Will found him dead. I'm not so sure Skull was the one that sent his goons. I don't have all of the details yet, but things are getting weirder by the minute," I huff.

"What the fuck?" Dallas says, his hands moving to rest on my thighs. "I've pissed a lot of people off, but Skull was the only one I know of that wanted me dead."

"You're assuming this is about you," I reply.

Dallas's hands tighten on me. His eyes grow hard. I can see his jaw working beneath the skin. I turn away not wanting to read too much into his reaction.

I need to keep everything in its compartment. I don't have a place for feelings. I need to have a baby and make it in this marriage for a year, without killing anyone. Love is not on the menu.

-B-

Dallas

I've always considered my heart a hardened place. I've never had reason to care about anyone. No one has ever given a shit about me. Yet, hearing the woman before me suggest she's the sole target for all of this has my blood boiling.

I've gotten into my fair share of shit, but I'm no killer. At least, I wasn't before I got married and started trying to get my wife pregnant. Now, I'd kill any motherfucker that even thinks about looking her way.

"What aren't you telling me?" I ask tightly.

She closes those pretty eyes and I can see the pain that surfaces on her face. I want to comfort her, but I can see she's finally going to open up. So I stay stock-still and wait.

"There's a time stamp on every entry to my property. Every keycard has its own signature which leaves a time stamp upon use. Aisha and all of my brother's except for one have a time stamp for that day," she starts opening her lids.

"But that's not the weirdest part. Aisha's time stamp lines up with the time she arrived for work. Which makes sense. She also left when we left, which is why she has no exiting stamp. All of the guys are logged in within seconds from each other which should be impossible, let alone unnecessary.

"If they arrived together only one would need to use their card. To top it off. They all have entry signatures but no exit," she explains.

"Which brother isn't logged in?"

"Will," she whispers.

I frown at the name of the asshole that knocked me out in the back of the van. I don't think either of us are fans of each other. Now, all I can think about is putting a bullet between his eyes.

"I see what you're thinking. Will can't be behind this. I just can't believe that. We...he wouldn't do this. But...," her brows knit. "It...it was his keycard that let them in when we ran."

"How accurate is this system?"

"It's tested weekly. Aisha and I built it ourselves. But…," her face fills with concern. "The gate, when we left it was sitting wide open. It shouldn't have been. You need to be verified through the keycards to get in or out. Otherwise, someone has to give you access from inside."

"I think for now, we hang low. You're safe here," I say.

"I'm going to kill whoever's behind this," she seethes.

"No…you're not. Not within the next twelve months," I say in warning.

"Fuck," she pinches her eyes closed and rubs them with the heel of her palms. "This is crazy. Someone is out to kill me and I can't do shit about it."

My anger rises and my mind starts to turn. The thought of my woman not being safe doesn't sit right with me. I don't care if this is a marriage of convenience. The moment she said I do, she became mine.

"Have you ever helped to train any of the others?" I question.

"Yeah, my youngest brother, Sebastian. Augustine made me train him as soon as he arrived," she nods.

"Is he as good as you are?"

"I'm the best," she gives a fond smile and nods again. "But Bastian is a close second."

"Then you'll train me," I say with confidence.

"What?"

Her mouth drops open and she looks at me like I'm crazy. I lift my chin as her eyes bounce all over my face. Yeah, I've fucked up a lot in my life, but there has to be a time when enough is enough. When you decide your tired of believing the bullshit people feed you and you show them you're more than they tell you, you are.

This is my time to do that. It's the only way I know how to repay her for what she's done for me. If she's as good as she says she is—which I believe she is after that night back at her place—she can teach me to protect her.

"There's nothing that says *I* can't kill for a year, is there?"

"No," her brows draw.

"Good, than you'll teach me," I nod.

"Dallas, I don't know," she says warily.

"You see something in me others don't see. You believe in me for some reason. I can do this," I reply.

"Have you ever held a gun," she side glances me.

"I'm a shit shot. My daddy always said I was too stupid to learn to shoot properly. I think he just knew I'd kill his ass if I could get away with it," I muse aloud.

I see something flash in her eyes. I know instantly her mind is made up. Her jaw sets, her eyes light with determination, her lips twist up with anger.

"We start in the morning. Five a.m.," she says sharply. "Any idiot can pull a trigger, but only a skilled genius can become what I'll make you."

With that she pushes up from her seat and storms from the room out the side of the house. I grin after her. It shakes something in me when she shows emotions for me—good or bad—they show she cares.

CHAPTER TWELVE

Focus

Havana

"Focus, Dallas. Again," I bark.

He shakes his head clear and glares at me. I can see he's pissed but I'm not letting up. His sweaty chest glistens in the hot sun as it heaves with his exertion.

"How the fuck am I supposed to focus when you just kicked the shit out of me," he snarls.

"Stop whining and do it again. You're bigger than me, but it doesn't give you an advantage unless you focus. Stop using your size and use your brain," I command. "Again!"

He charges me again, still angry, still unfocused. I climb his body like a cat, wrapping my legs around his neck and flip him to the ground with my momentum. He grunts with the impact of the fall.

"Fuck," he growls beneath me.

I shift to sit on his chest and stare down at him. His face is red with anger, frustration, and his efforts to take me. I'm sure he thought this would be a lot easier.

"Listen to me," I sigh. "You will lose every time if you move with your anger. Tune all of that shit out and use your brain. You're smart. Charging at me mindlessly will never work. I'm faster than you and I aim to sting. I'll hurt you before you can apply your size and force."

"You're a tiny demon from hell," he huffs.

I throw my head back and laugh. We've been at this for a week now. While he's taken to guns and using a bow and arrow, he has been struggling with the hand-to-hand combat.

Dallas has a street brawler style. That might work in a bar fight, but it would never cut it in my world and especially not with one of my brothers.

"Oh," I yelp, as my back hits the ground.

I look up into Dallas's eyes. They're just the way I like them, one blue and one hazel brown. I see the lust in his eyes as he looks down at my sweaty bust and exposed stomach. He licks his lips, causing a shiver to roll through me.

"How about I turn that laughter into a different sound altogether," he purrs.

"You just want me to stop kicking your ass," I chuckle.

He presses his hard length into me. Gaining my full attention. My core weeps for him instantly. Dallas has molded my body into a toy for his pleasure. His touch has become my one weakness. I'll just never tell him so.

Dipping his head, he pulls my nipple into his warm mouth through the fabric of my sports bra. My back arches up off the grass beneath me. I gasp when one of his hands snakes its way into my shorts.

I bite my lip and close my eyes as a moan releases from my lips. I forget all about training a new assassin. I get lost in the feel of his hands, mouth, and the scent of his cologne—mixed with his sweat—infiltrating my senses.

Dallas brings me right to the edge with his skilled hands. I'm ready to explode when he pulls his hand free of my shorts. I whimper in anticipation of him freeing himself to finish what he's started.

We've already figured out a few days ago that pushing my little shorts aside for him to gain access to my pussy works just fine. However, his fat, thick length isn't what I'm greeted with. Instead, his fingers lock around my neck cutting off my air.

My eyes flash open, my hands wrap around his wrist. I curse myself for being so silly. This motherfucker got me.

Never, ever let your guard down.

"You said to get my hands around your neck. That was the objective. You didn't say how I had to do it. I used my brain," he says with that sexy crooked smile on his lips.

"I'm going to kick your ass," I hiss.

"Not before I fuck you," he teases darkly.

His lips crush mine, his hands around my throat relaxing slightly. I claw at his sweat soaked back pulling a groan from his lips. To prove my earlier point, he releases one hand to shove his shorts down his hips, before pushing my shorts and panties aside to thrust into me.

My legs wrap his waist in a death grip as he pounds into me. Our teeth and tongues clash as he takes me almost frantically, as if afraid he'll never get the chance to again.

"Dallas," I cry out, pulling away from his demanding kiss.

My fingers claw down to his ass and dig in. I can't stop my hips from rocking against him for more. My juices are creating a wave for him to surf through.

He cups my face, forcing me to look at him. I've never seen him like this before. His eyes are drowning in so many emotions. I can't pin down a single one, but I think I see fear…sorrow…despair. A few others I won't dare acknowledge because I'm sure I'm imagining them.

"If it comes to your life or that money, fuck the money. You fight and you fight to kill. We'll be fine," he grunts.

I nod, not knowing what to say. His face tightens. I guess my silent assent isn't enough.

"Promise," he demands as he continues to pump his hips into me. "Promise me."

"Okay, I promise. I'll fight."

"Now come for me," he orders, giving my neck a gentle squeeze.

I explode all over him. It's so fast and hits me so hard, I'm taken aback. Dallas follows right behind me spilling his hot seed into me.

I need a moment to catch my breath and my thoughts. Dallas places his forehead to my cheek, his breath fanning heavily against my neck. My body starts to rev demanding another round.

Only, my mind and my body are met with disappointment as he slips from inside me and peels away to get to his feet. He doesn't say a word or look back as he makes his way down towards the private beach.

I sit up on my elbows to watch him as he goes. I have no idea what just happened. Collapsing onto my back, I look up at the sky.

Never, ever let your guard down.

~B~

Dallas

"Stop being so stupid," I growl at myself.

Seeing Anita beneath me with my hands around her neck triggered something in me. The thought of someone else doing the same thing—only with the intent to harm her—makes me see red. The anger pulsing through me is all-consuming.

I'm falling for her. It's the dumbest thing I've ever done in my life, but it's happening. The thought of her not fighting back because of some money locked away somewhere is insanity.

I'll protect her with everything I am, but I need to know she's going to protect herself if the need arises. Fuck that money and her asshole father for putting her through this.

I probably shouldn't have walked away like that, but I couldn't allow my emotions to be revealed. When this is over, Anita will go back to being Havana. She will return to the life that doesn't involve a fuck up like me.

I might as well get prepared for the rejection. The more I fall for her the further away from distancing myself I get. Typical me, setting myself up for failure.

I'm starting to believe in the image that stares back at me in the mirror in the morning. That's a dangerous thing to do. This Dallas isn't real.

Cleaning me up and slapping expensive clothes on my back doesn't change a thing about the core of who I am. While I'm foolishly falling in love, Anita is busy trying to survive and whip my ass into shape.

I need to focus on the goals here. Find out who wants to kill Anita, get her pregnant, collect my money, and go home. I'd be good to remember all of that.

CHAPTER THIRTEEN

Don't do it!

Havana

Five Months later…

I wipe the sweat from my face with a towel as I watch Dallas. His mind has been somewhere else, even as he's become more focused on training. He's getting better, a lot better.

I smile as I think of how far he's come in the last six months. Augustine would've seen a lot of promise in him. Dallas has potential in my world. I think he could be as good as me if he wanted to get serious about this.

He turns to reach for his water bottle and the tat on his back draws my attention. It's a single feather that looks as if it's falling down his back. It's the only tat he has but it's so detailed and realistic.

"What made you get that feather?" I let my curiosity bubble up from my lips.

He turns to me, then looks over his shoulder. When his eyes turn back to me I can see him debating on whether or not he plans to answer. He moves towards me, hovering over me when he stops.

"I once knew an angel. When she left, I swear she left a feather behind," he murmurs, reaching up to place a piece of hair behind my ear.

I go to ask more, but the sound of my cell draws my attention. I rush to pick up the line. Aisha and the lawyer are the only ones that have the number.

I'm hoping that Aisha has found something useful to help me understand what's going on back home. Seeing her number on the screen I become hopeful. However, when I pick up that all changes.

"Hello," I say into the phone.

"I need your help," she rushes through the line.

"What is it?"

"I...I've been staying at Rich's place. He went out with Will and Tristan last night. He never came home. I thought it was him coming into the apartment, but it wasn't.

"When I realized someone broke in it was too late to hide. I grabbed my purse and ran. They chased after me, but I think I've lost them for now.

"I'm scared, Havana. I don't know who to trust outside of you and Rich. What do I do now?" her voice trembles with her last words.

I try to think quickly. This isn't good. Aisha is the last person that needs to be in a position like this. I'm not there to cover the damage that could result.

I shudder.

Not knowing who to trust limits our options. I close my eyes, but against my better judgement I make a decision. It's for the best, at least I believe it is.

"Go to Feldman and Steins in the city. Tell them Anita Steel sent you. I'll have instructions waiting there. Watch your back. Make sure you're not followed," I say quickly.

"Okay, I will. Thank you," she says softly.

"Tell me you're not about to do what I think you are," Dallas grunts when I hang up.

"She needs my help," I reply while texting the lawyer instructions.

"Havana," he snaps getting my attention. He never calls me by that name. "This is insane. No one knows how to find you. We're safe here. You're safe here. Why bring her here? You can send here somewhere else."

"You wouldn't understand," I say.

"What I understand is that my wife and my baby need to be safe at all times," he says firmly.

"I'll be fine and so will the baby," I wave him off.

"Don't you do that shit to me," he points a finger at me. "You used to do that to everyone around you. Wave them off, telling them what to do. Talking to people like you run shit and they have to do what you say. I'm your husband not your employee. I'm telling you this is not a good idea."

"You're my fake husband," I seethe. "Aisha is my family. I'm going to make sure she's safe with me. She's not like the rest of us. This type of shit triggers her differently. I need to help her."

The moment the words fall from my mouth I regret them. I see the hurt that fills his face. In the last three months it's been us. We were so excited when we realized I was pregnant. Everything has been falling into place.

"I didn't mean it like that," I try.

He lifts his hands and backs away. His eyes harden and his jaw ticks. I feel like shit.

"Do whatever you want. I'm just the hire cock after all. What do I know?"

My shoulders sag as he turns to disappear. I want to follow after him, but I need to finish covering Aisha's ass. My chest pings and my eyes sting. Dallas will never know how much more he's become to me.

~B~

Dallas

It's been hours and I'm still stewing from her words. Finding out we're having a kid had me thinking of Anita as my family. That baby will have everything I never had. I wanted that to include a father that loves him or her.

How silly of me. My days are numbered. Anita made that very clear.

"Dallas," her sweet voice calls, cutting me through and through.

I don't turn. I continue to look out over the ocean view. If I look at her, I'll only be reminded how perfect she is and why I don't deserve her.

"Dallas, please," she pleads.

"What?" I huff like an asshole.

"I'm sorry about what I said. You have to understand—"

"I understand perfectly, sweetheart. Don't you worry your pretty little head about me. You do what you need to do," I cut her off.

"Don't do that. Don't shut me out," she says softly.

"I never let you in," I reply, getting up to walk away.

"Asshole," she hisses after me.

"Always. Never said I was anything more," I toss over my shoulder.

CHAPTER FOURTEEN

Guests

Havana

I've been in a foul mood for three days. I haven't said a word to Dallas. We've been pretending that the other doesn't exist. I know he's still pissed, but I'm just as pissed at him.

I've been feeling a little nauseous this morning, which isn't helping my agitation. Aisha should be arriving sometime today. I've tried to focus on that. Once she's here and safe I think I'll be able to relax.

Hearing a car outside, I get up from my desk in the study. I doubt Dallas will bother to show his face since he doesn't even want her here. I blow out a breath and shuffle my way towards the front door.

When I open it my mouth falls open. Tears sting my eyes as I look at Aisha's guilty face. The sting of betrayal cuts deep. Dallas had been right.

I back away from the door, my hands going to my rounded belly. All eyes follow the movement. A wide range of stunned and angry looks appear.

As I retreat, they all step over the threshold. I feel so stupid. This is what Augustine warned me about. I'm always so trusting. This has to be the dumbest thing I've ever done. I got emotional and let my feelings make a decision for me.

"You've got to be kidding me," Tristan grinds out first.

"You let that dirty piece of shit get you pregnant?" Will snarls.

"My wife and my baby are none of your fucking business," Dallas's voice booms.

I turn to look up at the top of the stairs where Dallas stands overlooking the scene before him. His guns drawn and pointed at my brothers and Aisha. His glare is hard and I can see he's ready and willing to pull the triggers.

"We're not here to harm her," Aisha says softly. "We came to help."

"You lied to me," I accuse.

"No, I didn't. Rich called me when I was on the way to the airport. Let us explain," she pleads.

"Don't you move," Dallas warns.

My eyes land on Will moving for his gun. I clench my fists at my t-shirt. I don't know what's going on, but I'm starting to get pissed.

"Baby, come here for me," Dallas says.

I turn slightly to see he's made his way halfway down the stairs his guns still aimed at our new guests. I back away from everyone, making my way to Dallas. He quickly places his body in front of mine.

"She's our sister. We're not here to hurt her or the baby," Sebastian says.

"We're here to protect her," Rich adds.

"From who?" I snap.

"Joey, Tanner, and Clifton," Theo replies. "We found them at your place that night. Joey claimed you called them. When you took off we knew something wasn't right."

"Why were y'all there in the first place?" Dallas snarls.

"Fuck you. We don't have to answer to you," Will bites out taking a step towards Dallas.

Dallas cocks the gun in his right hand. "I don't think you want to do that," he warns.

"Stop it. Both of you," I chide stepping around Dallas.

His arm goes around my waist, tugging me into his body. I don't have time to relish his warmth as much as I want to. I miss being in his arms, but I need to get to the bottom of what's going on.

"We'd been drinking and talking. We could see you were stressed out. We were tired of waiting," Theo says.

"We needed to get to you before you did something stupid," Will says glaring at Dallas.

"You weren't the only one to get a message from Dad. We think the only ones that didn't were those three and Aisha," Tristan says.

"Dad never trusted the three of them and well, we're still trying to figure out the deal with not sending one to Aisha," Rich continues.

"Aisha can't lie," I blurt out.

All my brothers look at each other and burst out laughing. Aisha starts to pout. I've only spoken the truth. It's how our father would think.

"Damn, I never thought of that. It makes sense," Rich chuckles.

"You, shut up," Aisha fusses at him.

Rich holds his hands up in surrender as he continues to laugh. Things are starting to fall into place and make more sense. I fume as I think of the three that we all considered family.

"We're still trying to figure out what those three are up to. I don't understand why they broke into Rich's place," Tristan says.

"Are you sure you weren't followed here?" Dallas asks.

"Who is this guy? Why'd it have to be him?" Will asks while glaring at Dallas.

"He's my husband. Get used to it. I don't have to explain more than that," I huff.

"Well, I think you do," Tristan says. "We found some old files of Augustine's. They have this guy's name in them."

"What?" Dallas and I say in unison.

"He had a birth certificate, social, and school records. All dating back to before he found Havana," Rich says.

My mind reels with this new revelation. What would Augustine be doing with all of that. My mind twists itself in a knot trying to figure it out.

"What I want to know is, why were you the only one without a time stamp entering the house that day?" Dallas snarls pointing at Will.

"What?" Will says in confusion. "The gates were wide open when we arrived."

"That's not what he means," I say. "I'll explain it all. Maybe you guys can help me make some sense of things."

"Look, it's been a long trip. Can he put those guns down so we can get something to eat," my youngest brother Sebastian groans.

"Shut up, Bastian," I giggle. "Dallas, you can put the guns down."

-B-

Dallas

I'm still not sold on trusting these people. Anita and the baby are my priority. I'll blow a hole through the rest of these fuckers if I even smell them cooking something I'm not eating.

Just like the steaks on that grill. I'm not able to sit back here in the yard and break bread with those assholes. I'm still not over being tased and punched in the face.

"You care about her," Aisha says as she walks up to my side.

"We were friends a long time ago," I reply.

"And they say I don't know how to lie," she snorts.

"You're in love with her. It's okay, I won't say anything. I think you two make a cute couple. She's very protective of you and you're the same way with her," she says.

I grunt noncommittally. I'm not in the mood to share my feelings. Especially with someone I don't know.

"Don't mind Will. He has a thing for Havana. She just never saw it. She's like that you know? She totally misses cues when a guy is into her."

"I'll keep that in mind," I grumble.

"You do that. I'd hate to see her miss out on someone loving her."

I turn to look at Aisha, but she's already walking away from me. I frown wondering if it's that obvious to everyone but

Havana. It still feels strange to call her that. They all do and she asked me to do the same while they're here.

"I don't know you, but I don't have a reason not to like you," a deeper voice pulls my attention.

I turn to find the youngest brother, Sebastian. He looks just barely an adult. I can see in his eyes when he looks at Havana how much he admires her. It's truly like she's his big sister.

"Then, I'd hang around a bit. I'm sure to give you a reason," I mutter.

"You're funny," he chuckles. "I'm going to be an uncle. It seems weird. You know? With what we do and all. I never thought any of us would have families and all that someday. Heck, Havana cusses like a sailor. I don't know if I can see her as a mom."

"She'll be perfect. She has a gift for loving people. She makes things brighter for everyone in her world," I reply.

"Shit, you are in love with her," he says, his mouth hanging agape as he stares wide eyed back at me.

"You have a good night," I mumble, turning to head back into the house.

CHAPTER FIFTEEN

Talk to Me

Havana

I noticed the moment when Dallas left the little barbeque my brothers and Aisha started up. I could see the tension in his body as he walked away. He never returned. My heart ached to go after him.

I've been thinking ever since. Never once have I truly questioned Dallas. If I can trust anyone, I know I can trust him. He was ready to protect me with his own life.

Any one of my brothers could have taken his life earlier and Dallas wouldn't have seen it coming. That didn't stop him from throwing himself in front of me and our baby. He did it without hesitation.

Normally this type of thing goes over my head. You know, me and guys, they're just not on my list of priorities. I miss it when one has feelings for me. Yet, in this instance I'm not stupid, I'm also not the only one in this relationship that allowed their feelings to become real.

I didn't follow the rules. I let my guard down and allowed him in. I blame it on being stuck here with him every waking moment over the past six months. Then there are my hormones that haven't helped things. I've been letting all types of emotions run wild.

I'm in love with Dallas. I don't quite know when it happened, but it has. As many times as I tried to talk myself out of it, I've fallen right off the cliff and I've done so happily.

From the way he looks at me, I know he's fallen as well. It's one of the reasons I'm so sorry for the words I hurled at him. He was right. I did put us all in danger.

If my brothers were out to harm me they could have succeeded because I put my guard down. I've become too comfortable here and I need to fix that, but first I need to fix this gap and the silence between the two of us.

I stand in the threshold of our bedroom watching him as he sits against the headboard with his arms behind his head. That scowl doesn't belong on his handsome face. The light casting in through the window highlights his strong features.

He's my own personal dark brooding angel. He's the true good one in the relationship. His foul mouth is his greatest sin. I've done way more things to be judged for. Yet, Dallas has lived a life of ridicule and self-loathing.

Why try to ruin such beauty? I've asked myself that question repeatedly. To taint such perfection is plain sinister.

His neglectful mom and hateful dad did a number on him. If only I could wash that all away as easily as I had the dirt and filth from that first day. I would give anything to give him a fresh start.

There's no hope for me and my crew. We were bad eggs from the beginning. I enjoy what I do. I don't remember a time before the joy of disposing of bad people.

Sometimes, I wonder if my parents were bad people. Had they been mean to me, causing me to be this person? I don't think I'll ever have the answers to those questions. I can only move forward from this point and the people in this room.

I move over to his side, kicking off my sandals before I climb on the bed to straddle his lap. His hands fall to my belly on instinct. He still won't turn his head to face me.

I reach to run my fingers through his hair, loving the feel of the silky strands as they sift through my fingers. Again, I note how gorgeous a man he is. Perfect in ways he doesn't even know about.

"Six hundred and twenty-one," I whisper.

He finally turns to me with knitted brows. I take a deep breath to still my nerves. It's time I make him understand.

"That's the number of kills I've made. I've been busy. I never take a hit that doesn't feel right. Augustine taught me to always follow my gut.

"I didn't do that when I brought Aisha here. You were right. I should have listened to you. That mistake could've gotten me killed. I'm not used to being told what to do.

"Augustine trusted me. I've called the shots and taken care of things for as long as I can remember. I've never had a partner. I'm sorry for what I said," I pause when he turns away from me again.

His jaw works as he absentmindedly rubs my stomach. I can feel the baby shifting at the same time. This is a big dose of reality. I love this man and I'm having his child.

"I hurt the ones I love," I murmur, grabbing his attention once again.

His eyes turn on me, his gaze super sharp. I can see him searching for the meaning of my words. I cup his face, leaning in to kiss him softly.

"Everyone knows it. When I get stressed, I lash out at those I love. I'm sorry, Dallas. You were right," I say.

"Don't lie to me, *Havana*. I'm not one of your marks and I'm not a gang of hitters you need to keep happy. You don't have to sell me bullshit," he husks.

I don't miss the fact that he calls me Havana or how harshly he says it. Almost like the name burns his mouth. I've learned that to him I'm two different people. I'm Anita and Havana. He tends to separate the two sometimes.

I tilt my head and study him. I see the pleading in his eyes. It takes me back to when we were little. I can't believe I have the memory, but I remember that look from when my last day of the summer would roll around. He would plead with his eyes for me not to go. When I would have no choice but to leave he would plead with his eyes for me to return.

"Why is it so hard for it to sink into that head of yours that I love you?" I huff.

"Because you've never said it," he breathes. "You always say what you mean."

"I love you, Dallas," I reply.

"So now you expecting me to say that shit back?" he says with no expression on his face.

My mouth drops open. My hands fall to my hips. I nudge him with my baby bump.

"Screw you, asshole," I hiss.

That breathtaking smile appears on his lips. Pulling his bottom lip into his mouth, he bites down on it. His hands move to my thighs, sliding up under the hem of my skirt.

"Ain't much I love in this world, but you are what I love the most. You've been shooting right through my heart from day one," he rasps.

"Does this mean you're talking to me now?" I pout.

"I'm about to do more than talk to you, Kitten. I'm going to talk to you, taste you, and fuck that little pregnant pussy until you come screaming my name," he croons.

"Here for all of that and then some," I purr, cupping his face and kissing his lips.

Despite his harsh words, he gently turns me onto my back, placing me on the bed. Looking up at my husband and his open look of love fills my heart to almost bursting. I palm his face as he leans in to kiss my lips, my nose, my chin. He continues to rain gentle pecks all over my face.

It's the most tender Dallas has ever been with me. He continues his path down to my collarbone. Tugging my shirt up he discards it, reaching to release my bra next. He stops to hover over me looking down at my body beneath him. His eyes linger first on my swollen belly then my breasts.

Leaning in, he kisses my stomach, over and over, landing his feather light kisses in a new spot each time. His fingers hook into my skirt and panties, peeling both from my body slowly.

His lips gently caress my hip, his tongue peeking out to play against my skin. I squirm as my juices start to make my crack slick. I can hear more than see him inhale. His tongue trails the underside of my belly.

"How could I not love you?" he murmurs, but it's so low I believe he's talking to himself. "It's the only thing I've done right in my life. Every time you're in my life things are right."

"Dallas," I whimper.

"Simmer down, kitten. I've got this," he breathes against my skin.

Spreading my legs and settling between them he positions himself to feast on me. I wish I could see past this belly. I love watching that intense look in his eyes when he's taking my body to places only he can.

I claw at the pillow beneath me, my right leg locks behind his neck. The act encourages him to really go in. Placing a hand to the headboard for leverage, I lift my hips and rock against him. His hands move to support my waist, pulling me into him as he does what he does best.

He devours me through two orgasms. I'm panting and damn near sobbing by the time he lets up. Dallas crawls up my body, turning me onto my side. His big body spoons mine, his hand grasping my hip.

He pushes into me tenderly. My heart stutters with the slow entry. His breath warms the top of my shoulder. He stills once seated fully, nuzzling my neck.

"I love you," he rasps. "All I want is to protect you. You don't have to be sorry. Just remember when I'm telling you something it's because I want you safe."

"I know," I nod. "I love you, too."

I feel the stupid tears gathering. I've been so emotional while pregnant. It's so out of character for me. My heart swells even more as I think of how I've been able to show those emotions with Dallas.

He begins to rock into me slowly, his hand moving to lace his fingers with mine. His leg slips between mine. I rest mine on top of his, rocking back into his slow thrusts.

Dallas's lips latch onto my neck. My head falls back against his shoulder. He moves our joined hands between my legs.

I bite my lip, my breathing coming through my nose. His free hand reaches for the longer strands of hair on top of my head, tugging back. The sting sparks through my body, causing me to grip him tighter inside me.

"Anita," he groans into my ear, licking the shell. "You always feel so good."

"You too," I gasp.

"Then, come for me. Show me how much you love me. Rain all over this cock. Make me yours," he croons.

I tighten my fingers on his and start to bounce back on him a little harder. His loud groan fills the air. Our sweat soaked bodies work together to reach the goal.

The tears start to flow when I understand what Dallas is teaching me. Whether he means to or not, he's showing me we work better together. He's been doing all he can to learn to fill in a gap for me.

When we both cry out together it's the most powerful and intimate climax I've ever had. We made it happen together. When I needed him to carry more of the load he did and I'd given him my trust the whole time.

I listened to his body and he listened to mine. From here on out we'd do this together. I need him more than I allowed myself to admit. Now I understand.

"I love you," he whispers pecking the side of my temple.

"Back at you," I grin and giggle.

He swats my ass and growls into my neck. I start to giggle more. His arms wrap around me, holding me tightly.

"Fucking smart ass."

"Asshole," I retort.

"Your asshole, kitten," he replies.

"Damn, right."

He chuckles and nips my shoulder. This feels better. This is who we've become in the last few months. This is our world. The others are just joining it.

CHAPTER SIXTEEN

Baby & Counting

Dallas

Five months later...

I'm exhausted. Why didn't anyone tell me having a tiny human was so rough? As tired as I am, Anita has to be three times as exhausted.

Our son is adorable. Never thought I'd be a part of making something so perfect. He's everything right about life, but his little ass has a set of lungs on him and boy, does he use them. I wish I could cry and get a tit shoved into my mouth.

If I even mention my cock, Anita looks like she's ready to chop it off. I'm treading lightly around her these days. She's actually counting down the days until she can kill again. Thirty-seven days to be exact.

I can't blame her. Our family isn't safe. Her three renegade hitters—because everyone refuses to call them brothers any longer—are still out there. For whatever reason, they want Anita dead and I can't have that.

I roll my shoulders and look down at my tiny son in my arms. Two months can go by so fast. With each day he starts to show more and more of a little personality.

"You keep spoiling him if you want," Anita calls out from the bed.

I look over my shoulder to see her laid out, arm across her face, legs every which way. I smile and shake my head. I thought she was sleeping.

"I didn't want him to wake you," I reply.

"That tiny monster doesn't care who he wakes as long as he's clean and fed. Why use guns when you could just place him in the center of a room and let him cry the place down?" she teases.

"Not a bad idea. I'll place him in Will's room," I grumble.

"I wish you two would cut it out. You're like two big babies," she groans.

"Why offer to help with my training only to piss me off every fucking time," I hiss.

"Twenty for the swear jar," she giggles.

I roll my eyes. We both promised to dial it back for little Augustine. Yes, as hurt as Anita was by her father's scheming, one look at our son and she wanted to name him after the only man she remembers as a father.

"Fine," I huff, moving to the table we keep the jar on.

"He's one of the best, Dallas. He wants to make you as good as we are. You still get emotional when you're angry. That's something we had broken out of us young. We all have been pushing at that weakness to help you learn through it.

"You just notice it more with Will because he gets on your nerves regardless. He knows and exposes it. Haven't you noticed how much better you've gotten. Your hand-to-hand has become stellar in the last few weeks. I'd send you on a job without a worry. You're ready for on the job experience if you ask me," she says peeking out from under her arm.

A scoff leaves my lips. I saunter over to the bed with the baby still against my bare chest. He's quiet, finally, snuggled into my warm skin. Getting on the bed and positioning myself with my back against the headboard, I look at my wife.

I love that she believes in me the way she does. It makes me want to make her proud, but I'm no hitter. I'm a man learning to protect his own.

"If the day comes where I need to protect you and this little guy, I'll be ready. But I'm no assassin," I say, telling her just as much.

"Um," she smirks.

I look down at Augustine, wondering what he'll be when he grows up. Leave it up to Havana and her gang, he'll have his first kill by ten. I've listened to the stories they've been sharing over the last few months. They all miss it.

"I know we have money, but I was thinking about getting a real jo—"

My words cut off. Both our heads snap up as the alarm for the main gate goes off. They won't hear it out there, but everyone inside the house has just been alerted. Tristan and Aisha designed the system that way while the others helped to install it.

"Take him and get into the safe room," I say handing over the baby.

"Dallas—"

"You just said I was ready for this. Don't argue. Keep our son safe," I kiss her forehead. "I'll come back to you. I love you too much to die or lose you. Neither is an option."

"Tanner is a follower. Easy target. Joey is a terrible shot. He'll force a fight whenever he can. His right side is weak. You hit and hit it hard, don't let up," she says, nodding her head. She licks her lips. "Clifton is a sneak, he's the one to watch."

I give her a nod of understanding. She cups the back of my head for a passionate kiss. I break it, not because I want to, but because I need her to get to safety with our son. She grabs her gun out from under her nightstand and starts out of the room.

"Havana," I call stopping her in her tracks.

"Yes," she turns to face me.

"If it's you or them, fuck that money," I remind her.

"I'm a professional, dear. I can wound without killing," she says with a wicked gleam in her eyes.

I shake my head, but I don't get to say another word. She takes off with Augustine. I go to the closet and start to load up. I toss on a bulletproof vest and holster. I grab a few rounds, four glocks and a rifle.

If you're going to come to the home of a hitter, knowing she has at least five others with her, you're coming prepared. I'll be just as prepared. After all, we have the element of surprise. A newly trained hitter with everything in the world he loves to lose. Who do you think will come out on top of this one?

CHAPTER SEVENTEEN

Sleeper

Havana

When I make it to the safe room, a wide-eyed Aisha is already there. I eye her closely. The last thing I need is for her to have an episode. Augustine realized too late that Aisha wasn't meant for this world. She's missing the switch the rest of us possess.

Augustine's other mistake was taking in those three bad apples. Joey and Clifton were always the hardest to reel in. Tanner was just like a little puppy wanting someone to follow. Joey was the first to extend a branch and he latched on. That will be his downfall.

To be a real hitter in our squad you have to earn your place, no one is just given anything. Those three never took to that lesson. The things you see when it's too late. It stings to think that those oversights may be behind Augustine's death.

"Are you okay?" I ask Aisha.

"Yeah, Rich said stay here," she says robotically.

I groan internally. She's already shutting down. *Shit.* This can turn into a really good thing or a very bad one.

Placing the baby down in the carrier, I grabbed on my way here, I check my clip and the chamber. The one time my son sleeps soundlessly is during a damn war. Yup, totally my kid.

I'm itching to be out there. I have a bullet for all three of their asses. Bringing this shit to my door not once but twice. Now with my son here. I'm fuming. I pace the floor as I keep an eye on the monitors. A smile curls my lips as I watch my men.

Dallas is making me proud. He's moving just like one of the boys. If I didn't know my man's frame so well I wouldn't be able to tell the difference between him and my brothers.

"Go, baby," I purr at the screen. "Yes, Dallas."

"Wow, he's doing great," Aisha drawls beside me.

"Yes, he is," I nod.

We continue to watch. My heart stops when I see someone approaching Dallas from behind. I lean into the screen willing him to turn around.

"Turn around," I call. I gasp when they fire in his direction. "Shit."

"He missed," Aisha states the obvious.

I frown, but I can't look away. I fist pump when one of my guys takes out the one that just shot at Dallas. I can't be sure, but I think it was Will.

They're back on the move. My eyes bounce across the monitors trying to keep up with Dallas. I growl when I find a camera with Joey's cocky ass. He's not even carrying a gun. I know it's him from the white blonde hair and his shorter stocky build.

"Just shoot him," I yell at the screen when I find Dallas at the edge of the clearing where Joey has appeared.

I hiss when I see Dallas taking the bait. I told him a million times not to engage when he doesn't have to. When he drops his guns I groan.

"Well, now you better whip his ass cause I'm going to kick yours," I snarl at the monitor as if he can hear me.

"Havana," Aisha gasps.

I reluctantly turn to her. She's pointing at one of the other monitors. It's the one that feeds right outside the safe room. I narrow my eyes at the sight of Clifton grinning into the cam.

This cocky bastard is worse than Joey. Clifton actually believes he can take me. It's a belief I've allowed. It was built into him purposely.

I lick my teeth, tasting the ass whipping I want to give him. My hand hovers over the button to release the lock. Augustine's tiny whimper halts me. I turn to look at my son, he frowns in his sleep before settling back down. I huff, turning back for the screen. I shift to tap the intercom instead.

"You made a big mistake," I seethe.

"You know, those were the same words the old man said before I took his life," Clifton chuckles through the speaker.

"You murdered him?" the words fall out of my mouth in agony and disbelief.

"I was never meant to be anyone's puppet, Sis," he croons. "You're younger than me. What do I look like following your orders? I got real tired of that shit.

"Then we had to let him handle our money. I'm a grown man. Why should I have to ask for money I've earned with my own bloodstained hands?"

107

"You greedy bastard. He would never deny you what was yours. He took care of us all, made sure we were okay. How could you?"

"Kings answer to no one," he bellows.

"What king? You're a fool," I fume.

"See that's the problem you don't even see the throne he set you on. You don't deserve the power given to you. I do," he pounds his chest. "I'm willing to paint the streets red in blood to get what's mine."

"Oh, you're going to get what's yours," I say darkly.

"I know I am. You followed his rules just like a good little girl. You see those videos were on his laptop. I know what he wanted you to do. You're all idiots. It never ends with him. You don't even see what's coming," he throws his head back and laughs.

"What are you talking about?"

"It doesn't matter. I'm going to kill you all and then I'll get to the money and start a real squad," he snarls.

"Let me out."

I turn towards the cold words. Aisha has tears staining her face. Her body is trembling. I can see Aisha is gone for sure.

Well, guess who just arrived at the party.

The others have always assumed Aisha isn't in the field because she's the weak link. Not so, she's the sleeper in the bunch. Pushed too many steps in the wrong direction and her switch is flipped. Augustine was always afraid of her inability to switch it back. When Aisha goes dark she goes dark. We keep her out of the field to keep her from losing herself.

"Taj?" I question.

"Let me out," she heaves.

"You've got it, baby girl," I purr. "Make that motherfucker pay."

"He was the only father I had," her voice cracks. "He saved me from eating garbage when I was only seven. Oh, this motherfucker is going to pay."

She walks to the door. I note she's tucked my gun in the back of her pants. I doubt she'll even use it. When Taj comes out she doesn't need it.

"Hey, bitch you hear me? Bring your ass out here," Clifton roars.

"Oh, you don't want that, Hon," I sing. "But I'm going to do you one better since you asked for it."

I unlock the door and release the hell no one but Augustine and I know exists. It's the reason she's my assistant and right hand. She may run the legit side of things, but she knows the other side first hand as well.

-B-

Taj

I was damaged when Augustine found me. He thought he could fix me like the others. He thought he could train me and give me an outlet for my rage and despair.

I was the one that was too broken for this work. When we go to work, I slaughter. We don't know who will come back from a job. My mind has too many pieces to hold together. We do well holding them together as Aisha.

She's the smart caring one. She couldn't lie her way out of a paper bag and hurting someone causes her heart chills. Not me. Rich hasn't met me. I don't know if he could love me the way he loves Aisha.

I don't give a shit about any of that. I've loved two people in my life, Augustine and Havana. They understood me enough to take care of all of me. Every voice, every broken part of me. They knew to place me back in my box and allow me to stay there.

The door slides open and I blink at the hot tears. I never liked this motherfucker. I plan to do more than slit his throat like he did Augustine.

"You?" he scoffs. "Why the fuck would she send you out here?"

I look up at him through my lashes, my chest still heaving, tears still flowing. He doesn't even understand that I'm not the shy assistant anymore. That's his problem, not understanding details and order.

"She would've just killed you," I say coldly. "You don't deserve that. I'm going to make you suffer."

"Bitc—"

"*Awwwww*," I cry out as I lunge at him.

I'm too fast for him. My blades slice at him each time he tries to block or attack. I prefer blades. I can hide them on Aisha in case I ever need to come out and play.

"What the fuck?"

He lurches as far away from me as he can get. A grin plays on my face as I continue to watch him through my lashes. I start to sway to the music only I can hear. Clifton looks at me like I'm crazy. He has no idea how much.

"You know, in old tribal cultures they danced at the ceremonies for fallen kings. Let's dance, Cliff. Your reign is about to end," I sing.

"Crazy, bitch," he growls, reaching for his gun.

I hold it up and laugh.

"You looking for this?"

"How—"

"If you wanted to take the throne from Havana you should have learned the kingdom. There are always sleepers. You don't even know how dangerous *she* is.

"Who were you taking shit from, boy? You wanted this shit, come get it," I snarl.

His face tightens. He starts to move around me, assessing. Bad decision. I move forward swiftly, dropping to the floor, when I slide through his legs I cut the back of his right Achilles and behind his left knee.

"Ah, fuck," he cries out.

"*Shut up!* Take this shit like a man," I roar back.

"I'm going to kill you," he hollers.

"When you get to hell, tell them Taj sent you," I retort.

He stumbles at me, throwing his weight on me. He's bigger than me. I stumble back a bit, but I don't go down. I cut across his stomach, before sending a short jab under his chin. I pierce just enough to send him leaking, not end his life. I want to drag his death out.

"Taj!"

Havana's scream reaches me right before I hear the gun fire. My smile grows. That's why I love Havana. It's family over everything. She deserves to run the family.

My back hits the floor hard. Clifton glares down at me. Pain explodes through my body.

"You don't deserve to live," I sob into his hate filled face.

CHAPTER EIGHTEEN

Church

Dallas

I made it down to the foyer of the house to find five blood thirsty men standing armed and ready. I could see in their eyes the same thing I saw in Havana's the night she killed those three men before my very sight.

I feel something tug loose within. I've seen a man killed before that night, but this is different. I'm protecting what's mine. I think I understand them all a little more. None of them are killers just to be killers. There's a moral compass that I've struggled to understand up until this point.

They kill for those that can't. They make the real devils disappear. They kill to protect the helpless and weak. I understand. I finally get it.

"He's awoken, boys," Rich nods, with a smile.

"Let that beast out, brother," Tristan pats my shoulder.

"This is the big leagues now, boy. Let's take these traitors to church," Will says with a sinister grin. "Shoot to kill."

All five men release a loud sound, somewhere between a bark and a roar. With that we move out the front door, down the driveway, into the wooded area. We've done this in drills over the last few months, but this time feels different.

I have a son and the woman I love back in that house. I feel the moment I forget Dallas, the fuck up and I become Dallas the husband, father, and hitter. I become one with the task at hand. Kill until there's nothing left to kill.

Movement to my right draws my attention. I turn looking through my night scope and fire. I catch my first target in the forehead. A satisfied smile tugs my lips, but I don't have time to celebrate.

I keep moving and firing. All of our guns have silencers, even the rifles. Sebastian is a weapons specialist. He's altered or enhanced most of the weapons.

I can hear the shots from the other side, but my team moves in silence. The silence becomes my comfort. The more of it the better, it means my side has this under control.

I have an eerie feeling coming from behind me, I turn to find the source. I stare at a barrel of a gun pointed at me and freeze for a second. The gunman's head explodes just as I snap out of it. I look to my left to see Will with his gun pointed in the direction of where the dead guy was standing only moments ago.

He nods at me and takes off. I refocus and move. My determination turns up. That was too close. I toss the rifle, pulling two pistols instead. I move to the edge of a clearing in the trees. My eyes narrow as a stocky blonde reveals himself. His hands in the air.

I know from the pictures Havana showed me, this has to be Joey. I know I should just shoot him. Everything Havana said about him already proves to be true.

He'll lure me into this fight because gunplay is his weakness. He's the weak link in the squad and he hates it. Kicking my ass would feed his ego, but what he won't expect is that I'm ready for him.

I drop my guns to my sides and step out into the clearing. I can hear Havana's voice hissing at me in my head, but I have something to prove to myself.

"You're as dumb as you look or that pussy has you feeling like a God," he taunts.

"You'll be praying for God to get my ass off of you," I reply.

He snorts, rolling his shoulders. His eyes casting over me dismissively. I grin, I've been under estimated all my life. I thrive off that shit now.

"I'll kill you and then I'm going up to that house to finish what I started. That bitch is the only thing standing in the way of my taking over. They listen to her because she has the money. When I control the cash then I'll control them."

"They listen to her because she's family. Money has nothing to do with it. I think you missed a few lessons," I retort.

"I have a lesson for your ass," he growls.

He comes at me fast and hard. I block his first combination, spinning out away from him. He recovers and charges again. He's a few inches shorter than me, with a shorter reach, but there's power behind his punches. I eat a few just to gauge him.

My father has dealt me more than enough blows to the head and body. I suck the hits up, while clocking this guys speed. He shouldn't be so sure of himself in a fight either. He might have been better off with a gun.

It gives him a false sense of comfort, as I've yet to go on attack. He goes for a roundhouse kick, revealing my opening. I spin and throw my right elbow into his right side, followed by a left upper cut.

He stumbles back but I don't let up. I spin to land a kick to his right leg and a quick follow up to his already aching ribs. I can see in his face he's stunned. He was expecting a totally different type of fight from me.

"That bitch you're talking about is my wife. I'd watch your mouth if I were you," I hiss.

His eyes light up.

"I'll be sure to gut that bitch until she screams. I might even fuck her before I finish her," he taunts.

I see what he's doing but it still hits its mark. My nostrils flare and I get ready to charge him. The only thing that stops me is the voice of the one person that knows how to push all my buttons.

"Focus, Dallas," Will growls. "We don't do emotions."

Anita's words from earlier come back to me. I rein in my feelings and focus. My jaw tightens as I get my head into what I have to do.

"You're better than him. Beat his ass," Tristan yells.

I crack my neck from side to side. It hits me that for once in my life people are calling out to my strengths, not my weaknesses. Anita isn't the only one to see me and my potential.

"You're one of us. Something he'll never be," Will bellows. "End this shit."

I turn my emotions into fuel. I work through them like Anita said. I move as if I'm going for his left and he goes to counter. I spin to his right and attack from that side before he can adjust.

And. I. Keep. Pounding.

An elbow to his head, a punch to his throat, a left to his ribs, a right to his gut. My knee revisits those ribs breaking a few without question. He pulls a knife, but he's in no shape to use it. I kick his right knee out and go for the kill. A roundhouse that has all my anger built inside it.

Anger for my no good parents. Anger for my wife and son having to hide away from this piece of shit. Anger at the world for always pushing me back when I tried so damn hard to move forward.

I take his fucking head off.

His headless body falls to the ground in slow motion, landing on its stomach. My chest heaves with satisfaction and triumph. We'll see what bitch he's going to kill now.

"Now, that's what the fuck I'm talking about," Tristian calls.

"Havana can pick 'em as good as the old man. I didn't see it at first," Rich nods.

"I took down Tanner. Anyone see Clifton?" Sebastian says.

"Motherfucker, they were all distractions. *Move*," Will barks.

"Let's go, we need to get back to the house," I demand.

We all move quickly to head for Havana, Augustine, and Aisha. My stomach twists with fear. Just as we reach the front door, shots ring out from the direction of the safe house. My blood runs cold. I pray life hasn't laughed in my face again.

"No," I roar, taking off for the safe room.

CHAPTER NINETEEN

No!

Havana

One, never trust an assassin. Two, never let your guard down. Three, don't allow your emotions to drive you.

Taj and Clifton did all three. Clifton had another gun he pulled when she was lost in her agony. He leaned on her to get the close shot. I saw it coming.

They said I couldn't kill, not that I couldn't shoot. I always have another gun. This one just happened to be strapped to the bottom of the baby carrier.

I got the cleanest shot I could take. I hit that sneaky bastard in the shoulder, right beside Taj's head. The force sent them both over as he placed all of his weight on her.

"You alright," I ask as I kick Clifton's body off of hers.

I note the sorry groan that comes from his lips. Taj looks up at me and nods. I know that look in her eyes. She leaps up and

sits her ass right on top of Clifton's chest. Grabbing a hand full
of his hair, she slowly drags her blade across his throat.

It's not the sight of her actions that's disturbing. It's the look
of glee in her eyes as she does it. She actually licks her lips as the
blade slides. When it reaches the other side, she shifts the blade
in both palms and begins to repeatedly stab him in the throat
and eyes. A smile on her face the entire time.

"What the fuck?" Rich breathes as he comes to a running
halt beside Dallas.

They both look on with shock and horror. Bastian, Tristan,
Will, and Theo are just steps behind them. I tilt my head to
watch Rich's reaction. I figured out what Aisha was trying to
hide from me.

Rich blinks at the woman he's been sneaking around with.
Awe and disbelief are written across his face. Mind you, not
much shocks us around here when it comes to violence.

"Aisha?" Rich mutters when she sits back on Clifton's chest
to admire her work.

"Aisha isn't here at the moment," Taj purrs.

"The fuck," all of the men before me say in unison.

"I'll explain," I sigh. "Taj, hon. Thank you."

Her eyes slowly leave Clifton's lifeless body. She stares into
my eyes for a few beats. I see the sadness that enters them.

"She's not coming back anytime soon," she informs me.

"Yeah, I figured, Love. It's okay. We're family. I've got you,"
I reassure her.

"I know," she nods, turning to look at Rich. "I hope
everyone can learn to like me."

"Holy fuck," Tristan breathes.

"Hi, I'm Taj," she waves sheepishly at Rich.

Rich pulls a hand down his face before giving a small nod. I can see he's speechless. I was the first time as well.

Yup, things have only just begun to get interesting around here. What in the world has my father left me with? A squad of crazy hitters.

My family.

CHAPTER TWENTY

Happy Home

Dallas

Three months later...

"You sure she's going to be okay?" Dallas looks behind us as Taj walks away with the senator's right hand.

Some jobs deserve to be messy. The betrayal of sleeping with a man's wife and stealing from his campaign places this job up there. The request was for it to be as painful as possible.

I nod towards the shadows, causing Dallas to follow my gaze.

"He'll never let her out of his sight," I say with a smile.

"Now that's love," Dallas shakes his head. "That girl is crazier than a bag of squirrel dicks."

"What?" I burst into laughter.

"Can we go home now? I've had enough of this monkey suit and this damn contact," he complains.

"Actually, I have one more job scheduled for tonight," I smile.

"You're kidding right?" he huffs.

"Nope, You'll enjoy this one. He's been staring at my ass all night," I purr.

"No way. Brock Rushing," Dallas lifts a brow.

"Crisco, placed a request a week ago," I shrug. "He's the main reason for this little get together."

"I actually won't mind this one at all," Dallas croons. "What's the plan?"

I reach up pulling my husband's head down to mine. He's hesitant for about five seconds. All else forgotten, he takes over the kiss. His hands go to my ass as I tug him towards the room I stopped us in front of.

Dallas kicks the door closed behind us. I push the jacket from his shoulders. His strong arms band around me lifting me into the air. I wrap my legs around him, wiggling so the hem of my dress lifts up higher to release my thighs. His warm palms move to assist, pushing the fabric up.

He breaks the kiss, his eyes blazing at me when his hands meet my bare ass. I give him a wicked smile. He bites my lip and pulls. When he releases it, he licks it to soothe the sting.

Dallas turns to sit on the ottoman at the foot of the bed. I grin at him, crawling back out of his lap. I unfasten his belt, not taking my eyes off of him. His face tightens with lust.

I reach to pull his pulsing erection out of his pants. He jerks and throbs in my palm. I lick my lips, eyeing the prize before me.

Hearing the sound I've been waiting for I grin. Dipping my head, I stick my backside in the air. Dallas reaches to knead my ass cheek as I start to lick the tip. He releases a low groan.

I let my saliva drip to cover him. The look in his eyes spears me on. I lick him from root to tip and repeat, drool...lick...drool. I pop my lips on the tip a few times before taking him to the back of my throat.

"Shit," he hisses. "You're going to make this hard."

"Mmm," I moan and grin around him. He pops from my lips and I look into his eyes. "Just focus and get it done."

He rolls his eyes, reaching behind his back at the same time I do. In one swift motion, he pulls his gun, placing a bullet through the throat of our peeping guest. I use the gun I pull to reach across my body and place a bullet through the middle of his eyes, only turning to glance over my shoulder for the shot. I turn back and smirk up at my husband.

"Perfect," I purr when I hear the body drop behind me.

I drop the gun at the side of Dallas's thigh. As if nothing else matters, I suck him back into my mouth. Fully intending to finish the job. Says a lot about the both of us because he doesn't stop me.

I bring him to a roaring finish. Licking him clean, then sucking my lips free of any leftovers. I stand, wiggling my hips to pull my dress back down.

Dallas reaches to tug me down into his lap. He grasps my face, taking my lips in a hard kiss. As if I didn't clean my face enough he gives it a good licking, sucking my lips into his mouth.

"Taj isn't the only one starting to scare me," he mutters giving me a crooked grin and side glance.

"Yeah, you should probably talk to someone," I tease, nodding my head at him.

He gives a full belly laugh and it looks good on him. His eyes sparkle with it. He's been so carefree since we've returned home.

"So, this life is working out just fine for you, right?" I chirp.

"Just fucking peachy," Dallas purses his lips and shakes his head. "No kills on our properties."

"But the cleanup is controlled," I pout.

"Havana," he warns.

"Okay, okay," I huff. "No more kills on this property."

"Why do I even bother?"

"Because you love me," I coo.

"Yeah, I do," he shakes his head. "Says something about me. Let's clean this shit up."

"Nope, that's what the cleaners are for. See, controlled. You still have a few things to learn, Dear."

"I never applied for the job," he mumbles.

"None of us ever do. It has a way of finding us."

"How convenient," he snorts.

"Yup, it is," I nod.

"Crazy."

"Crazier than a bag of squirrel dicks," I throw my head back and laugh.

Not Over

Dallas

I stare at the computer screen wondering if I really want to see a message from a dead man. I was shocked when the video appeared in my email, addressed to me from Augustine Knight. It took a few seconds for the name to click.

I've been debating on whether or not I should call Anita in to watch it with me. She's bathing the baby and I'm not sure what's on this video, I think it best to watch it alone for now.

I blow out a breath and hit play. The recording comes to life and an older man comes up on the screen. He looks familiar, but I chalk it up to seeing it in a photo in Anita's office.

"Hello, Dallas. If you are watching this that means I've met my demise and my little Havana has done well. She did exactly what I knew she would," the man on the screen grins.

"I'll never regret the trick your father pulled that night. I'd been beyond pissed to find that little girl in the car and not you. The bastard, I had a mind to come for you anyhow.

"I would have too if not for the accident. Anita's handlers were high out of their minds. Your daddy must have paid them in drugs. She was so small and badly hurt.

"I did what any human would have done. I took her to get help. When I started to dig into her life and found out who her parents were and the shitty life she had, I decided to keep her. That aunt had already sold her off in your place.

"Your father took the money I gave him for you and gave that woman crumbs for Anita's life just to spite me. Anita couldn't remember a thing, but she asked for you repeatedly. It was then that I knew I'd get both of my assassins. All I needed was patience.

"The years ticked by and our little Anita became my fierce Havana. She was the best of the bunch. I chose poorly with a few of the others. I realized that error too late. I thought to come for you then, but I could see the trouble brewing in my little family.

"Family, it can be tricky like that. Your daddy was the fuck up in ours. He was lazy and not even the money could get him straight. He kept you to spite you, not to keep you from who I'd make you.

"I watched you grow into a man and the start of your own troubles. I knew I couldn't talk you into our life without your back against the wall and I still had that little problem rising.

"This was my way of finishing what I started. The world has a need for us, but even we have a need for love and normalcy. I learned that the hard way. I didn't want that for Havana.

"I thought I could sit both my girls out. Havana and Taj were my heart. I took care with them, but they both come with their own corks. Havana's…she'll never be happy doing anything but being a hitter. At first my plan was meant to force her out of the life. Then I realized I just needed to show her how to balance it.

"So here we are. Welcome to the family, Dallas. Once a hitter always a hitter. I just regret not getting to train you myself. You showed potential from the moment I met you.

"Good luck with the squad I've left the both of you. They are a surly bunch. And son, remember me. I'm the essence of who you are. Steel wasn't your mama's maiden name. It's our real family name," the old man says just before the video goes dark.

Well fuck me.

ACKNOWLEDGMENTS

Remember Me is another one of those books that woke me out of my sleep. Dallas appeared telling me his name and demanding a story. I have to say I'm happy for it. It was a mental break I needed. I love these two and look forward to more from their squad.

To the ladies that joined me in New York for the 2018 retreat. I hope you enjoyed this book. Thank you so much for coming out and supporting me and my craft. I love what I do and being able to share it is a cherry on top.

I want to thank all of you awesome readers out there. You give me life. Thank you. Again, thank you for allowing my brain to process as it feels is best in the writing of every book. Your patience is appreciated more than you know.

Thank you, Lord, for placing a fire under me to hone in on the vision and to keep moving forward even when it's not all comfort and roses. I'm blessed just by your Grace and I appreciate the uncommon favor. Thank you is not enough, but praise is what I do. To Your Glory it is all due.

Where to next, Blue? *The land of Lincoln and the Blacks, Love. Hold on tight.*

ABOUT THE AUTHOR

Blue Saffire, award-winning, bestselling author of over thirty novels and novellas, writes with the intention to touch the heart and the mind.

Blue hooks, weaves, and loops multiple series, keeping you engaged in her worlds. Blue and her husband live in a house filled with laughter and creativity, in Long Island, NY. Yet, the city still calls to her to come on back for a visit.

Wait, there is more to come! You can stay updated with my latest releases, learn more about me the author, and be a part of contests by subscribing to my newsletter at www.BlueSaffire.com

If you enjoyed Remember Me, I'd love to hear your thoughts and please feel free to leave a review. And when you do, please let me know by emailing me TheBlueSaffire@gmail.com or leave a comment on Facebook https://www.facebook.com/BlueSaffireDiaries or Twitter @TheBlueSaffire

Other books by Blue Saffire
Placed in Best Reading Order

Also available....

Legally Bound

Legally Bound 2: Against the Law

Legally Bound 3: His Law

Perfect for Me

Hush 1: Family Secrets

Ballers: His Game

Brothers Black 1: Wyatt the Heartbreaker

Legally Bound 4: Allegations of Love

Hush 2: Slow Burn

Legally Bound 5.0: Sam

Yours: Losing My Innocence 1

Yours 2: Experience Gained

Yours 3: Life Mastered

Brothers Black 4: Braxton the Charmer

Coming Soon...

Brothers Black 5: Felix the Brain

Brothers Black 6: Ryan the Joker

Brothers Black 7: Johnathan the Fixer

Other books from the Evei Lattimore Collection Books by Blue Saffire

Black Bella 1

Destiny 1: Life Decisions

Destiny 2: Decisions of the Next Generation

Made in the USA
Middletown, DE
19 July 2019